Tea for the Rent Boy, and Other Stories

Tea for the Rent Boy, and Other Stories

Helen Lynch

Wild Harbour

First published 2018
Wild Harbour Books, Glasgow, UK
www.wildharbourbooks.co.uk

ISBN 978-1-9997189-2-3

A CIP catalogue reference for this book is available from the British Library.

Typeset in GT Sectra

FOR KOSHKA AND MIRIAM

Helen Lynch teaches Medieval and Early Modern Literature, as well as Creative Writing, at the University of Aberdeen, and plays in all-female ceilidh band Danse McCabre. Her first collection of stories, *The Elephant and the Polish Question* (2009) won the Bluechrome Prize. As Director of the WORD Centre for Creative Writing, she programmes its annual literary festival in Aberdeen each May.

Contents

The Mintie Wifie

I DECIDE TO COME TO SCOTLAND ON THE chance, you know, because my school-friend, Ola, she is here. There is no jobs for me in this moment in Poland. I want to explore in my life, not to be sitting always in same place in same job, waiting all the days for some boy who is not wanting me. So I come in this country. I sit in the top of bus riding to my home and I hear all around me the Polish voices – only sometimes the Scottish ones, and then I am not understanding one word.

In our flat are six persons, not always same ones. Ola's uncle arrange for us the flat with citycouncil. It's quite the nice flat actually. Ola is sharing the bedroom with me, and in other bedroom, and on sofa and on floor, is sleeping six boys from Wroclaw. Ola is being waitress in Caledonian Hotel, and these boys is working on building of railway station. In flat under our flat is not so nice group, drinking all day in park and selling pictures at doors. They tell to the people that they are poor Polish art students and that this pictures are original, even though they have many copies. Ola is somewhat knowing them, though I tell to her we are educated persons and don't have to know such as this.

There are many Polish in this city. I have friends and so, but I am keeping apart from them, the big groups. I come because I am wanting to be in this country, not eating only the Polish food from Polish supermarket and gossiping and watching who is doing better, who is making the money, getting the better flat than others. This is like our parents' generations, all this gossips and jealousness. I am not wanting this. I am not wanting neither that I get married and have the baby and everything will be all right for me. The Polish

3

here, they are not at home but they likes to complain everything is better in Poland – but in Poland they complain and they don't want to live there. This is a little bit our character, I think.

The light is bittie like on Baltic sea. When I am the small child I go there for my holidays. It is very high kind of light, the clear one, you know. When is raining, all this grey buildings is looking like concrete – it's really no difference – but, when sun is shining, all is sparkling, and all this towers and pointing and decorated parts is like the crazy castles. For person what was studying for six years the Architectural Design, is very interesting city, it's true.

Place of my work it is in citycentre, in square of tall, grey, quite old houses which is offices for advocates and other types business. Inside that place, everything feels like there was never interruption, like such calmness and quiet working was forever without never any break or startling at all. The carpets is grey, and worn only in the nice way, like from repeating the same walking since many years, and the blue walls is looking so respectable to me. This never interrupted respectableness of the colour, and everything about that building inside it and out of it, is saying me same thing.

I never was in such place where I knew this so clear. In Poland the money it is the new money, with glitterings and big cars – but in between was time when there was not this money and this powerful families of aristocracy like before: it was stop. For a whilie it was stop. This is when my mother go to the university with extra points for that her father was coal miner. The children of these aristocrats and intelligentsia didn't want to go for the university in this times, my mother said – they said was full of the dirty peasants. But she went – she was becoming the dentist, the first one from her village – and, because of her, I went also, for studying the architectural studies.

So, now is the new kind of study for me: I am cleaning the slate fireplace and I learn such new English words like 'wainscot' and 'mantelpiece', and 'skirting board' and 'cornices'. 'Chandelier', it's the same in Polish of course. 'Fender'– it's my favourite one. And in this office, where I am tidying the bureau and emptying the basket for the waste papers, is Mr Birnie.

I know completely from the get-go that he is liking me, Jim, Mr

Birnie. He is gallant to ladies like the old men are in Poland, and he can speak my name with good pronouncing the first time. And he tell to the others, Mr Anderson and Mr Reid – 'it's like cloud, not claw – Klaudia.' Even so, they are never succeeding to it. Probably he told even Joy, Mrs Cowie, but she is never talking to me with my name. I think in first moment that he is very tidy and smart man, with this tweed waistcoats and white, waving hair, still quite the thick ones – what we say in Polish 'stary kawaler', the old bachelor. Only Polish men are kissing the ladies' hands like that. He has the very soft-like, pink skin. Later, when he talk to me about in the war-time, I am doing all the time this calculation, that for sure he was older than he was looking. I thought was not possible he was near eighty years old. He remind me somewhat my Dziadek, my grandfather, although my Dziadek is much more sick. Mr Birnie is one of partners before Joy and Mr A., and even Mr R., but he is coming now only two days in the weeks for doing some small works there. He has still this wee office which I am cleaning the most slowly, for that I like to talk, and he also.

Unless Joy discover us, and she is giving this looks, and Jim says 'we'd best be getting on, quine, eh?' Mrs Cowie, Joy – her parents were having the sense of humour when they give to her this name, in my opinion, but of course no one thinks their child will turn out in this way. Mr R. and Mr A. are always called Mr R. or Mr A., but Mrs Cowie is always called Joy, as if she was the friendly one. Factually, she is the very bossy woman. She speak to me like I am the ten years-old child – but in fact I am soon noticing she speak to everyone in this way – well, maybe not the Mr Birnie. Mr Anderson is the shy and skinny man, and Mr Reid is fatter but also the very serious one. Neither these men is ever looking at me exactly in my eyes.

Joy is all the time enraging about the spaces for parking – every day she is red and shouting on this theme (Scottish are very crazy with cars, in my opinion). In centre this square is the places for parking of peoples working in businesses office. They are paying the small pounds for reserve this parkings. Once was time Joy discover some one person has parked car in her space and she was blocking them with her big four-wheels-drive car. The mannie for this car-parking, he was sending in the young man to say the apologise and beg for letting his car to come out. Mrs Cowie keep him to wait outside her office during twenty minutes for making him very sorry. She talk to *him* like the *five* years-old child. Only Mr Birnie was winking and saying to her – 'you did pretty well there, eh, Joy? Only three pounds a month for the moral high ground.'

This joke was not the easy one for me neither. My English is not so good. I am from the Silesian part, so in the school was more important the German studies, I think. Mr Birnie he have quite strong for me the Scottish accent and he must to ask me often 'D'ye ken fit that means, quine?' He was joking with me a lot because I have the troubles to understand, but he speak very slowly and I am getting the custom to it. And often he is asking me to speak Polish and to explain the words for him also. He is knowing long ago the Polish wifie, he tell me, so he remember also some words. Sometimes he is having the voice of Edinburgh like Mr Reid, but his voice it is all the time changing when he tells about being the fairm loon when he was the young one in not far country village. He laugh when he tell about the Polish airmen what come near to there in war:

'The quines were a mad for them,' he say me, 'wi their hand kissing and their clicky heels, and their waltzing ways. Fair loathed them, we did – or the older eens did onywey.'

He didn't to ask me, but I tell him I have not the interest in boys in this moment. Only one of boys from Wroclaw is even the bittie interesting. Pawel is somewhat not like this others. He has the mastersdegree in the Chemical Engineering. He doesn't to speak much, but I think he is pleased to himself fine well, and, when he *is* saying, he is very strong in the opinions.

Since I am spending the time with Mr Birnie, he start to remind me so strong my Dziadek. He is like him kind, and he move him the hands in same way, the very definite one – especially when is folding newspaper. My Dziadek was many years in coal mine and he is stopping to smoke only last two years, so he has the troubles to breathe well. He live now with my parents on the flat on eighth floor, but he like to read *Gazeta Wyborcza* and he fold it just the same like Mr Birnie. Also, way he is stroke the edge-part on his cup with just one finger when he is drinking the coffee, and moving always the head upwards before he start the speaking. This actions they are telling about the man of this generations, I think it's truth, no? The country it does not matter. I like this. Mr Birnie was the child during war, he told me, but my Dziadek he was with partisans when he was the twelve, thirteen years-old boy. He was never speaking about the past times, what was out there in forest. But Mr Birnie he tell to me many things.

* * *

It was really the awful dreich weathers – quite terrible really. Down was falling this sleetish rain – was not like the proper Polish snow – and it was even foggy, with this sharp flakes of the coldness coming in the straight lines to the face and in the eyes out of this grey colour of nothing to see. The buildings was also grey of course, like usually, so you had to shut the eyes really to walk in the street. Everybody was walking like this – no one person could to see the others or nothing, and only succeed not to crash one into others by guessing about the shapes.

On this day only me and Mr Birnie is managing to arrive for the work. In suburban part was real snow and no cars are succeeding to drive. We are coming first on bus – me from my flat and Mr Birnie from the small bungalow – very, very slowly, but we are arriving in final moment. Mr Birnie say I should to drink coffee to make warm and then I should to go home – and he make me this coffee, the very nice one, in his office. So now I ask him first time about this Polish wifie what he mention one or two time before – quite often actually – and he say he will tell about this story.

'Her name wis Leokadia, and she lived outby Mintlaw – that wis anither village near tae mine. She came fan the Polish airmen did because her husband was wi the forces right enough, but he wisnae an airmen then, ken – he'd been taken to Germany wi a lot o ither men tae work. She hid a wee daughter, jist a few months ald fan she first came, and she worked that bit fairm wi jist a couple o local loons that wid stay wi her six months; an the priest for the Polish airmen, he wis billeted there an a, which is mebbe why folk didnae gossip sae much as they micht, ken?'

His voice was change – he was become the fairm loon, like he

7

always say – but it seem to me I understand him better than usually.

'Jist a couple o times, fan she wis fair short o money I reckon, she cam doon tae oor mairt and sold sweeties she'd made. Mint creams, they were – and awfu fine. My Ma kept sayin how peppermint essence wis awfu hard to come by, but mebbe she'd stored some up – though some folk said she made it from the spearmint in her garden. Some were white and some were green – brushed wi chocolate – just a bittie taste on each one. Naebody hid chocolate like that. Folk said she'd a friend doon in London – or a fancy man in Peterheid. They were wrapped in waxed paper and cut oot in shapes like hearts and mushrooms and moons, and some like spades and clubs and diamonds – like playing card suits, ken. The minister wisnae right keen on that, as I mind. Well, somebody ca'd her "the Mintie Wifie". Fae Mintlaw, see?'

I did not see at all, not for some moments after I nodded for showing that I did, but I was not wanting him to stop, even for explaining me.

'The name stuck and she wis aye the Mintie Wifie efter that. We young loons thocht we wis rare wits tae think o that, ken? Leokadia – folk hid a rare job tae chaw on that, ken, and as for Skrzypczak, weel .... naebody could thole that, nae wey. Like I said, a the Scottish lassies were fair wild for they Poles, wi their braw uniforms, their fancy moustaches an their nice manners – they kent how tae talk tae the quinies, ken? Some o them even read poetry. O course the quines wid niver hiv looked twice at a lumpish loon like masel – I wis a bittie ower young, ken – but I could see the situation right enough. A the unwed mannies, those in reserved occupations in the fishing and the fairming, they fair hated them, the "great mincing mullokers" as they ca'd them – though they were fine enough laddies itherwise, and they could drink right enough, they'd grant them that.

'Onywey the boot wis on the ither foot wi Leokadia. A the lodgers who worked for her, or the few servicemen billeted there later on, wis efter her. She'd a cloud o black hair and a fine way wi her they a said – and her baking and cooking were fair legendary. They niver got onywheer, mind – she wis married – never made ony bones aboot that. Even efter the war, fan news came through that her mannie wis last heard o in a Labour camp in Dortmund, and fan the Reid Cross, efter two mair years o lookin intae it, wrote tae tell her he'd died there. She and the bairnie bade. They took on help in the summer and for the tatties. I wis jist seventeen fan I went first for the tatties and bade on while December.

'We folk are odd aboot the things we want – oftentimes, we don't want at first fit turns oot tae be the maist important – and want sae much fit, a few years efter, we can barely remember. Certainly, I'd nae idea aboot the Mintie Wifie save the braw memory o they peppermint creams. I didnae ken how it happened – I hardly kent her at a, nor onything aboot her but fit I could see wi ma ain eyes, yet soon I wis that mad for her.... the wey she put the plates oot, brushin her hair from aff her brow wi the back o her fist. The wey she wid carry the bucket, or her face fan she wis sewing a button ontae Irenka's jacket, or fan she'd read her leather-bound books some evenings, and try tae explain to me fit wis in them. Classics o Polish literature, she tellt me – some kind o historical poems, it seemed maist like, wi lairds and ladies on braw picnics in pear orchards, or novels aboot Romans. She wis ayeweys kind and a bittie condescending – as if she wouldnae forget ma age – but she wid smile on me like she couldnae help hersel. Why wis I nae goin on wi studying fan I'd done sae weel at the Academy? Did I want tae spend my life howkin tatties?

'Fan she spoke, it wis like she found the Scottish sounds she hid tae make that harsh that she'd tae put mair breath intae them, and they came oot wi a lang, saft rasp. In that voice wis everything I wanted tae find oot aboot life and the world, a the things I ever wanted tae ken aboot anither person. There wisnae ony time in her life she tellt me aboot fan I didnae love her, or ony she could tell me aboot fan I widnae love her. Fan she spoke aboot life in Poland afore the war, or fan she wis growin, I loved her every moment o her life.

'Irenka – aboot six she must've been fan I kent her – a coarse wee thing oot the hoose and that well behaved at hame. A the bairns taught her the bad words in Scots and she didnae ken at first. She ayeweys sat atween us an looked at us, fae ane tae the ither, while me an hir mither wis gowking like a pair o dafties, wi that much tae say we couldnae utter a word. It sent me fair daft – sometimes oor fingers touched the handle o the same spoon or the cover o the same

9

book. Father Jerzy wis ministering for the new Polish Displaced Persons camp at the old army base at Dufftoon, as well as the airmen and their families roon by, so he wisnae there a the time, but there wis Bob Murison, fan I first came, and later his brither Geordie. They wisnae meant tae bide in, but she'd often tae mak them a bed doonstairs next tae mine on the floor.

So it wis rare enough I wis there on ma ain wi jist her an the quine, an even then I wisnae sure, apart fae the gowking, that she'd ony... till the nicht we wis eating her beet broth and there wis something odd aboot her, like she widnae bend her heid fan she wis sat doon at the table, a bittie shame-faced. In the finish I realised fit it wis – in a that cloud o black hair she'd hid mebbe three or fower grey eens, and that day she'd pu'd them oot.

'We sat roon the table, and it wis snawing – early December it wis – and the winter previous hid been the worst on record. This een hadnae been sae bad, but it wis fair snawin and blawin that nicht, and fan we heard it – cough, cough, like that, cough cough – ootwith the windae, we thocht we wis dreaming. She passed me the ladle for the broth and I thocht of how, later on, fitever happenend, I wid kiss her. Cough cough – it cam again aboot five minutes efter – though, wi the wind blawin, the rattlin o the door wisnae really a knock. Still, I got up tae see fit it wis, the door fair dinged me back intae the room, and a wraith o a man in a cap and grey overcoat, a blackened wi wet and plootered wi snaw, fell across the doorstane and intae ma hands. She seen his face and she said "Henryk."

'Twa things I saw – I saw her keek at me, jist the one look, like a stricken bird full o the shot, fan it lies in the marsh grass and flaps and it's best tae wrang its thrapple. And I saw her eyes rest on her mannie wi nae love or even recognition, as we helped him tae the settee and took aff his droukit coatie that wis mair a piece o rag. But even in that look I saw the pity on her. I went oot then, tae fetch in the coke for the fire, and fan I came back Father Jerzy hid been ca'd and the new arrival taken upstairs tae the bed.'

'Did he die then,' I asked, hoping it, 'if the priest was come?'

'No, quine, he didnae. It sounded worse than it wis. Jist a fair dose o bronchitis. I've a bit o trouble that wey masel nowadays. Bronchitis,' he said again, tapping on his own chest where the waistcoat is having the button.

'But she was loving you.'

'Aye, quine, she wis, but you and I ken fine well it's nae enough.'

* * *

I had to go back to Poland during some weeks because my Dziadek was died. The economical situation is not so good now and most of Polish is leaving. Mr Birnie was died while I was in the Katowice for funeral of my Dziadek. Ola was thinking she will to lose the job – it's not even truth but there was much gossips. She go only one time selling those false pictures at doors with this social dregs from flat below. One woman is not believing – Ola is all time blushing when this woman start to ask the suspicious–like question. Someone is calling to the crimestoppers and police is visiting in our flat. Ola's uncle he arrange for her to go back to the Poland. When I came back I discover first about the Mr Birnie, then about Ola.

At first I was not wanting to stay neither, even though I was lucky and I still have the job. It is not nice any more in my work – everyone is sad. Even Joy was crying in her office and her face is many times red even these weeks after. He told me he did not live for the long time, this husband of Leokadia, maybe three, four years, but during this periods he, Mr Birnie, was gone away to Edinburgh for studying with the law.

'But you still remembered her,' I said him.

'I remembered her right enough.'

This was this kind of man who will love you for whole of the lifetime, you know, even though he miss the chance. I am still not understanding why he is having to miss the chance – it make me somewhat to enrage actually – but he did it, and he didn't to forget. We Polish and Scottish, we like this kinds of tragedy – tragedy of not to have what you wants – and we understands the other.

Then I am thinking about this Jim, Mr Birnie, and how he was carrying in him always some part of Poland, and because he choose to tell about this story I am holding also some part of him. And besides this, I didn't to visit yet this famous Mintlaw. Pawel was offering before to take me there on his motorcycle. It might be I will to get job in Caledonian Hotel, now is no more Ola and my

11

English is much better than before. I come to Scotland to have the new experience. Maybe I will to go to Mintlaw with this Pawel with the big opinions. Or maybe I will to go with only myself.

Overnight Observation

SHE WAS AWFUL GROGGY WHEN SHE CAME ROUND. The nurse lifted her off the trolley into my arms, taking care to avoid knocking the boxing-glove bandages that covered her hands. Her blue dressing gown was fastened by the top button like a superhero cloak but otherwise she was naked, except for her nappy. I wanted to warm her, though she didn't feel cold. For a moment I held her in front of me and we all looked at her – Ross, the nurse, me – then I climbed into her bed. I left Ross to do the explaining and snuggled her in the crook of my arm.

And there we stayed. When night came we were wheeled regally through the corridor into the night ward. The consultant was a bit concerned, he said, about the amount of mucus on her chest. They'd rather keep her in for observation, just tonight.

'I'll have to stay with her,' I said quickly. 'She's still breast-fed.'

Of course I was very welcome to stay. There was a day-room just along the corridor where the mothers usually found the chairs relatively comfortable.

'I'd rather be in bed with her, if you don't mind. She always sleeps with us at home.' I risked the confession – she was one-and-a-half, after all – but he didn't seem inclined to mess with me.

Ross left me with a sandwich he'd bought. Kirsty was still sleeping, though she'd woken briefly and suckled. I lay and thought of her and of my relief. The operation itself was minor. I eased myself away from her enough to sit up and start the sandwich.

There were other kids and their parents in the ward. The boy in the bed next to me had just been told he'd have to stay another night. He was scowling into the hand-held computer game his Dad had given him, glaring his tears into its small screen and fiddling with the knobs.

His Mum said it wasn't so bad. He'd be asleep all the time. They had to go home, for Stewart, see. They'd stay otherwise. The boy looked at her as though he couldn't believe she existed, scowled down at the screen again. His Dad had been trying to say that there was nothing for it but to try and put up with it another night, that he'd go home tomorrow for sure. Finally he told him to stop bleeping that bloody game.

As soon as his parents had gone, he flung the game on the bedside table.

'No need for that, Matthew,' said one of the nurses coming on duty. 'He still here?' She asked the other two nurses, jerking her head at Matthew so that they turned round.

Most of the children on this ward had had tonsillectomies. At the far end a girl with long, pale hair was being sick into a bowl. On the other side of the ward a mother with immaculate lipstick and an expensive-looking checked suit was trying to quiet a whimpering three-year-old who wouldn't lie down. A nurse told the woman to go to the other room, that she'd settle the child. The mother did as she was told, though her look as she moved away from the bed conveyed a mixture of relief and doubt. In the cot directly opposite a wee boy, even younger than Kirsty, was getting his parents to take turns on his toy phone.

The large screen at the end of the ward was showing The Lion King. Kirsty woke up, sat up, looked at her bandaged hands, lifted one, then dropped it as though she had forgotten it already.

'Cheese,' she said, looking at my sandwich. 'Mummy eat cheese and bread.'

I was thankful she was such a good talker, that at least she could tell me what was going on with her. I fed her most of the sandwich and gave her a drink of water. She seemed quite enlivened and turned at once to the screen: stampeding animals, the wicked lion clawing at his rival at the top of a cliff, the fall, the thundering hooves, the dust, the trampling, the lion cub nuzzling the immobile body of his father. I felt suddenly distressed. Why did they put this stuff on?

Kirsty was riveted, her pupils huge. I tried to distract her with books, with her toy mouse, to pretend that nothing very important was taking place on the screen, but she wasn't fooled.

'What that lion do?'

The wee boy in the cot opposite was vying for her attention. His parents were half letting him and half shushing him, as though they would dearly love some company and entertainment for their son but couldn't be seen to seek it. The child seemed in a gregarious mood, yet in this open room full of people whom he was clearly dying to get to know, his parents seemed all the more careful to keep to themselves, not to impose.

So I took Kirsty over and at once he wanted her to play telephones and involved her in a book-swapping game, while I chatted to his mother. Calum had a testicle that had started to work its way in the wrong direction. His operation was the next day but he was in overnight to help him to fast.

Eventually Calum and Kirsty grew so spirited that they wanted to run up and down the ward, so we took them out to let them charge about the corridor. Shyly, remark by remark, the other mother and I probed one another, each trying not to look more or less permissive than the other, aware of the eyes of other people and of the authority of the institution, whose representatives strode periodically along the machine-polished floor.

* * *

I woke up certain it was day. A trolley was making its way along the ward. I got up and poked my head out through the curtains. The face of the clock above the door at the far end said two o'clock. Not possible. The orderly with the trolley offered me a cup of tea. I took one – I might as well be up for the rest of the night. I felt quite wide awake already. The night-nurses were clustered round the desk in a pool of light. Two had their backs to me. The orderly gave them tea.

I'd already drunk some of mine and felt jittery straight away. The orderly was friendly but not chatty – though I felt sped up and ready to talk – and she soon moved on to other wards. I sat on the edge of the bed and sipped some more tea.

I lay and listened to the noises of the night beyond my curtains.

15

I thought of the humps in the dark beds and closed my eyes, but at this point Kirsty stirred and started rooting for my breast. I turned myself towards her and eased the nipple into her mouth. She was not suffering at all, I thought, glorying in it. This was a normal night for her, smell of Mummy and warm milk coursing down her throat in small, satisfied gulps.

Someone cried out, a faint, strangulated, dreaming cry. Then another voice was calling, desperately, but as if it hardly dared be heard.

'Nurse, nurse.'

The pale-haired girl at the far end. There was the unmistakable sound of someone being sick – a sound I knew retrospectively that I'd heard several times in my sleep. Perhaps no one had heard her – should I call from my bed to alert someone..? Or could I ease the baby..? – but the clipped tread of one of the nurses proceeded down the ward. There were sounds of gulping and more retching, the puke plootering the sides of the bowl and, to judge by the tutting of the nurse, the front of the child's nightie as well.

'Look at the state of you. D'you think we've endless supplies of fresh nighties? You'll hae tae make dae with that one - here, dab it wi' this.'

She was about eleven, I remembered, with a clammy face, her long hair dripping down the side of her face like melting wax. I saw her in my mind's eye, a few droukit wisps at her temples, eyes still watering from the effort, blinking, swallowing the bitter remnants down her swollen throat.

The boy in the next bed was moving fretfully, scissoring his legs, thumping his head down on different parts of the pillow, mumbling. One of his covers fell off and I pulled my curtain back on his side and peeped at him.

'Och, leave him,' one of the nurses at the desk told the other, who looked as if she might do something. 'He's aye the same. Stop that, Matthew,' she commanded, and they went on with their conversation.

I'd seen the one with the iron-filings hair register that I was watching. Was this normal for them? I slid my finger into Kirsty's mouth to try to break the suction on my breast. She was fast asleep and barely sucking, but she detected the attempt at once and lunged at the retreating nipple and began sucking for all she was worth. Matthew was not an appealing boy. His dark, skinhead cut emphasised the rectangular shape of his face, and gave his pallid skin an almost purple tinge. He was not cute and biddable and he did not want to be there.

The third nurse was back again to join the other two, but almost immediately had to return to the other end of the ward – just as she reached for her cup. The girl was being sick again.

'You'll never be out of here with this carry-on,' the nurse informed her. 'Doctor says you cannae go home unless you keep something down.'

The girl sobbed at this and said something inaudible to me, bringing the explosion. 'You dinnae need your Mum, a great girl like you. Your Mum's at home asleep in her bed, which is where you should be too – you never will be if you won't try to keep your tea inside you. You'll be needing another operation if you go on this wey.'

Above the sound of the pale girl's sniffling, suppressed so that it turned into a cough so painful it came out as a yelp, and Matthew grinding his teeth, came the full-throated wail of a much younger child. I thought: this is what Hell sounds like.

The three-year-old had woken. One of the nurses went to her and, to my surprise, spoke to her quite kindly.

'Did you hae a dream? Come on noo, lie doon. You cannae sit up that wey?' The child clearly would not cooperate, but the nurse remained patient:

'Here then, hae some juice. The doctor says you're tae hae plenty of juice.'

There was a brief silence, during which the child seemingly took a couple of sips of juice from a tippee-cup, then went back to crying in a heartfelt but directionless way, as if she didn't quite know where she was. Quite suddenly, as if by a revelation, she summoned all her woe in a single yowl:

'Mummy!'

'You cannae hae Mummy. Here, hae some of your nice juice,' the nurse responded, trying to poke the spout of the tippee-cup between the child's teeth. The child continued wanting Mummy.

'Why can she not have her Mummy, for God's sake?' I thought. 'She's only down the corridor.'

'Open your teeth. Hae some nice juice. You're tae drink it.'

The child opened her mouth to wail 'Mu...,' the nurse tipped the juice, the child spluttered, choked, knocked the cup with her hand.

'There, you've got it all... that's a bad girl... you've wasted your juice. Well, I'll get some mair – you're tae drink it all. Doctor said. Mummy said.'

'Mummmeee ...'

'Mummy's nae here, she's gone tae work, she's sleeping. You dinnae want tae be a bad girl and waken Mummy.'

The child had settled into a hoarse and rhythmic screaming. Another nurse arrived as reinforcements and there were a few moments of struggle:

'Here, you get her arm... no, hold her,' the child by now terrified and hysterical. 'Noo that's enough! What a bad girl to waken all the girls and boys.'

Tears streamed down my face. 'She wants her Mummy, for Christ's sake. Why shouldn't she? For the love of God, go and get her fucking Mummy.' My head was screaming so loudly that it took me a moment to realise that I had not bellowed the words in actuality. I was frightened lest Kirsty should wake up into this horror, yet I felt the pull pull pull on my breast that seemed to go on forever. Should I offer to go and fetch the mother? Should I just do it? I didn't actually know where the mothers were exactly. What if I left the room and Kirsty woke up, as in this noise and disturbed atmosphere she was almost bound to do, woke to find me not there, cried out, drew the attention of the nurses...? Were I to intervene they would know at once what it meant, what the stakes were.

To my amazement I succeeded in disengaging myself from Kirsty. By this time, several other children in the ward were clearly awake. I had to sound reasonable. I presented myself at the child's bedside:

'Would you like me to run along and get her Mum?' I suggested helpfully.

The nurse who had the child locked in what seemed like a full Nelson looked over her shoulder:

'We'll settle her. There's nae need.'

'I'm sure if I was her Mum I'd want fetched,' I persisted, thinking of the check-suited lady. The second nurse looked at me. She knew a power struggle when she saw one, but she also saw that I was no real opponent for her. Without knowing anything, she knew I was not ready, and her voice was gritty:

'You bide there. We'll sort her oot, never you mind.'

The wee girl was quieter now, partly from exhaustion. The smallest whimper from behind Kirsty's curtains and I slunk back to my bed, while the child's crying went on, though softer now, for another age as I suckled my baby, shielding my own flesh and blood in my arms.

There was a brief lull. The nurses gathered again at their table, drank their cold tea and got quite chatty. I eavesdropped shamelessly, straining my ears, hating them, convicting them on every word. Pensions was their main subject, schemes for getting the best possible one, comparing arrangements they'd made, their husbands' pension options and so on. One, it emerged, was married to a policeman, another to a prison officer.

A wail from the cot opposite: Baby Calum. This time I was prepared. I would tell his mother, come what may. I *knew* her. Yet they fell on him, crowing, exclaiming, scooped him out of the cot and bore him off to their lair by the desk. Fortunately, he seemed quite happy with all the attention and only rarely showed signs of returning to grief.

'You're bonny, y'are *so.*'

'I see you. I see you, smiler.'

He was passed from lap to lap – 'Come tae your Auntie Jean' – as they went into raptures over his blue, blue eyes. What a handsome boy he was with that blond hair and those eyes. What a fine-looking mannie he'd make.

I lay in the bed, fists clenched, but Calum seemed to have dozed off on one of their shoulders, if their cooings of satisfaction were anything to go by. I relaxed a bit, just as one of them said:

'I think his nappy's wet, Jean.'

There were sounds of nappy-patting. I was scunnered. Who would wake a baby they've just got to settle, for *that?* Sure enough,

Calum objected robustly to the nappy change. Still, at last he was quiet and back in his cot.

Matthew was still tossing about, muttering and feverish. Another blanket fell to the floor. I got up and went to his bedside, replaced the blanket and put my hand on his hot forehead.

'Dinnae bother wi' him,' a nurse advised me from the desk. 'He's full o' trouble.'

'I'm sure he doesn't do it just to be annoying,' I said levelly in my best 'I know just what you're about' voice, turning my head to look at them, I hoped meaningfully.

Matthew was sleeping more calmly, but I'd not been back in my bed five minutes when the slightest sign of renewed restlessness had two of them at his side. They'd better things to do than wait on him all night, they said.

'Why did you nae tell us you was wanting the toilet?' one of them demanded. Matthew was barely awake, but they yanked him into a sitting position.

'I *doant*.'

'You do so,' said the other, and together they had him under the elbows, swung him out of bed and frog-marched him to the toilet, he protesting as the door banged shut. They didn't come out for a long time. He was still crying when he got back into bed.

On the other side of me, a girl of about five started to moan. I pulled the corner of my curtain back:

'Shh, sweetheart, shh,' I whispered. 'Go back to sleep.' She turned to face me, gave one wide-eyed look and dozed off.

'Oh thank God,' I thought, and must have slept. Another trolley. More steps, the light a rinsed-out version of the night-time grey which in hospital passes for morning. The day-nurses were at the desk, two ridiculously rosy-cheeked, fresh-faced young women, one sporting a plump, squishy chignon, the other a glossy bob, looking like teenagers from an Australian soap. A benign-looking older woman was moving among the beds, perching on the ends, asking the children about their cuddly toys, 'cheering them up'.

Kirsty seemed perky and content with her surroundings, toddling after the older nurse to display her toy mouse, then over to call on an equally cheery Calum, whose parents looked ill-slept and apprehensive. I resolved to clype to the snub-nosed doctor with the upper-class accent whom I'd already seen bounding with youthful efficiency around the ward. She wore her white coat unbuttoned so that it flew out to both sides and her stethoscope bounced on her chest like a string of pearls.

I started to explain. Was I making a complaint? Was I seeking some particular outcome? I focused on Matthew. She looked at me tolerantly, but with faint bemusement, stopped to remove a bit of fluff from her cashmere sweater, and assured me that it was her understanding that Matthew *would* be going home, subject to examination and provided he'd eaten breakfast.

'Well, if it's in the balance at all, please bear in mind what I've said. Your night staff really aren't very nice to him and I'm sure he'll get better a lot faster at home.' With this lame ending, I shuffled off.

Kirsty had found an older girl willing to build towers for her so she could knock them down with a swipe of her giant paw. Matthew was the only one still sat at the table in the day-room, two triangles of toast on the plate before him. Kirsty dived into the Wendy House. I squatted beside the boy.

'I know it's awful sore but you've got to do this to get home. Let's count while you swallow, then it won't seem so long.'

He nodded and took his first bite. It took ages but we counted each mouthful down.

Ross arrived, the doctor gave the all-clear and we went to the foyer for our taxi. Sitting on my knee in the car, batting her father's upheld hands with her boxing glove bandages and crowing, was our baby, intact. No trauma for her, apparently. Yet my insides ground and juddered with every gear-change, every jolt of the car, and there seemed no surface cool enough for me to lean my forehead on.

Sapozhkelekh

AUNTIE GOLDE SAYS TO PICK UP HIS BLANKET and be quick about it. Auntie Golde is quite fierce. Mummy says it's called strick and once she says it's old fashion, but I think it's fierce like the lion picture in Ruthie's book where the mouth and all the fangs is popped up. I'm not fraid of Auntie Golde either cause I'm the Eldest and so I don't fall asleep in cars or be fraid of grownups or pictures. Once Ruthie was so fraid she tried to tear the lion picture out and put it in the toilet. Most grownups like it if you do a really big smile with all your teeth. They like if you do what they say and don't ask questions. The question they specially don't like is why, but that's what a question is. Daddy specially doesn't like are we nearly there, and Mummy doesn't like is there anything to eat when she's already told you.

Auntie Golde says I'm standing there dreaming, but I'm not I'm just thinking, but she doesn't wait for me to splain her and she has picked up BabyDaniel and his face is over her shoulder with big surprise eyes going to the stairs. BabyDaniel is my brother and he's only one year old. Ruthie can only say bruvver cause she can't speak as well as me. Most of the time she followsmeround and is quite noying, though she is good for characters in games. I'm the main character cause I'm the Eldest but Ruthie can be everyone else. Usually Ruthie doesn't speak to grownups but I can do talking and she can say *and me* so that she gets everything the same as me. I'm the Eldest and I don't need a carry on long walks and I have to look after her so she isn't lost and leftbehind even if she's very noying.

BabyDaniel's blanket is on the armchair so I grab it quick to take for Auntie Golde. I wish I could stay down in the kitchen where Auntie Renka is. Ruthie is on the big stool that BabyDaniel's high chair goes on top of. Mummy says it's her perch. I can see Ruthie through the doorway where the light is all yellow. Auntie Renka pops pieces of honeycake in your mouth when you don't even ask her, and sour cream and berry jam on a spoon. BabyDaniel's blankie is scritchy and yellow, though it used to be white onceuponatime and it has a smooth, shiny feeling along the edge and a pointy corner which BabyDaniel likes to suck. Mummy says that colour's called cream, but cream is white like milk is. Ruthie and me call it his wee-wee blankie and we say it smells of wee-wee and is yellow like wee-wee and he's a baby and wee-wees on everything, even up in the air, and he has nappies and it takes everyone a lot of time to look after him.

Ruthie and me got cited and telled Auntie Renka bout the wee-wee and she laughed and we jumped up and down at the same time as the washing machine noise and shouted wee-wee blanket wee-wee blanket every time we jumped. Auntie Renka's name is Auntie Renya and Auntie Iroosha and she calls wee-wees shoo-shoos. Auntie Renka even likes questions and makes long answers to splain us. Her voice is funny and goes up and down like hickory dickory dock and she says funny words like Hennchen and Malootka. Ruthie can't say words like that cause she can't say Le sounds. She says maootka and when she has to say lollipop she can only say o-i-pop and once she said oddiplop and we laughed like drains. Daddy said it was her first el even if it was in the wrong place and should be cedebrated. Then all the grownups and me laughed like drains.

When Mummy and Daddy went away for a whole day and a night and a next day, I asked Auntie Renka why? But why? Why do they have to go out? She said Mamas and Papas need to rest sometimes. But they can rest *here*, I said, and Mummy can take a pill for her sore head. Auntie Renka gave us some honeycake which was very extra lishous. Ruthie says ishous. Auntie Golde did a big noise like a pig sneeze. Auntie Golde isn't noyed by questions she just never answers them. She says things or goes away, but she always notices your haviour, specially the not talking kind. Even when she's not looking.

Daddy says get that look off your face, my lady, but Auntie Golde says, what are you, a jug? I don't know what kind of jug she means.

24

Auntie Renka always makes a funny tishing noise at her with a bit of laughing. Auntie Renka has pretty white hair and it's not a bun. Her hair is bouncy and she has paleblue glasses on a dangly golden chain, but Auntie Golde's isn't and her glasses are on her nose.

Now Auntie Golde says over her shoulder – 'Don't stare. Bring that blanket. You help me a little, no?'

Mummy says that babies have wispy hair. I asked her why didn't the Aunties have any children, but Mummy said not everyone has babies. Auntie Golde and Auntie Renka are Mummy's aunties too but they're not her real aunties asamatterofac. When Mummy was learning to be a teacher before we were everever born she lived in their house, which is called Swiss Cottage even though it's a flat.

Once when Mummy and the Aunties were discussion and I was staying very quiet so it wasn't bed time for me, Auntie Golde said Poe lax in an almost shout, and she spitted like that, even onto the carpet. I had to go to bed allofasudden, but I asked Mummy what Poe lax is, and she did splain me bout it, but it was a funny reason.

The War was long ago but Auntie Renka and Aunte Golde were children then but not so little like us. The War was very bad and there were soldiers and people shooting like in films. Our Nana calls them fillums and we always laugh like drains so she says it again and Ruthie says she's funning us. Mummy says in The War it was very dangerous and the Aunties lived in a country far away called You Crane, though they weren't friends then and didn't know each other at all.

Mummy says it was very dangerous in You Crane in The War and all the neighbours were called Poles. Auntie Golde's family had to run away in a special bus, but the neighbours all stood in their front gardens. With flowers in? Yes, with flowers. What kind? I don't know, sunflowers, and dahlias – she was starting to get cross so I said Auntie Golde was in the bus? Yes and the neighbours made a horrible sign with their fingers on their necks to show they thought Auntie Golde and all her family were going to... weren't going to get away, and they were laughing. Even the children. I thought about the children laughing like drains in among the flowers.

But Auntie Renka had nice neighbours and some of them hid her in their barn for two whole years, even though she had to eat potatoes all the time and the rest of her family went somewhere else on a big train. Some people were very brave, Mummy splained me, Polish people, and other people, they hid people away even though it was a big danger to do that, and some people, they... they didn't.

'They laughed in their gardens,' I said. 'Laughed like drains.'

'Yes.'

So only Auntie Renka but never Auntie Golde is doing chitchatting with Mrs Dobramilska in the shop where they have the curly sheep horn rolls. Auntie Renka says the Poles are a Proudandfearlessnation but I don't know what that is. And Mummy says the Aunties have greed to disagree. She also says Nevverthetwain shall meet, but I don't know who Nevverthetwain is.

When we are at Auntie Golde's and Auntie Renka's I say to Ruthie let's pretend we don't live here, that we live at our house. Pretend the settee is our real house and we're just visiting. Leopard's visiting too, I tell her. Yes, and Old Ted. When Ruthie goes into a room she always holds Leopard up and shouts 'Eppard's here' and everyone laughs. Daddy says he's a faymus beast. Leopard has one green ear where something got spilled on him that wouldn't come out. We give them some pills for a sore head cause they're crying. Then they're all outofsorts so we give them two spoonfuls of medasun instead.

Leopard was gived to Ruthie when she was a teenybaby by Auntie Kathleen – Ruthie says Auntie Katheen and she's a real auntie of ours. She always comes to visit us with our Nana on the big train from Liverpool but we don't go there on the big train to visit them anymore since BabyDaniel was born cause it would make a nightmare. At teatime Auntie Renka said bout Granma but we don't have a Granma only a Nana. Auntie Renka said she didn't mean our Nana but there's a diffrunt other Nana too. I think this Other Nana lives more far away but Auntie Renka says this Other Nana lives in London so I say can we go and see her? Can we? And Ruthie says *and me*.

Auntie Renka says I'm sorry, Hennchen. My name is Helen but Auntie Renka says I'm hennchen but it's not a mistake, it means little hen. Auntie Renka says that the Other Nana is ever so Lishous. Auntie Golde makes the sneeze noise and says it's a unforbiddable thing, but I don't know what that is. In our house there is a picture of us with our Nana, Daddy and Auntie Kathleen at the seaside at More Come. We are eating sandwiches and I have a bucketandspade. Our hair is blowing into our mouths and our eyes are shut. There isn't any sea, only sand. The sea is farfar away. There isn't any picture of this Other Nana.

There's a picture of Mummy and Daddy getting married in a place called Turkey, like the bird Ruthie calls gobblegobblers. Mummy has short hair and a summer dress and looks very pretty, and Daddy doesn't have his glasses on. Mummy is writing in a book and Daddy is watching her. I can see from her mouth in the picture that Mummy has a concertration face on. Mummy and Daddy worked in a school in a town and the big children's mummies and daddies gave them boxes of oranges for a present. Uncle Harry and Auntie Jean are Mummy and Daddy's friends from the Turkey School. I like Uncle Harry cause he always swings us roundandround. He's always funning us and he funs Daddy too. When he comes to our house Daddy says hello you Proddy Barster and Uncle Harry shouts hello you Feenya Get and Mummy always laughs. Auntie Renka calls Mummy Reevka and sometimes hennchen too though her name's not even like Helen at all. It's Becky same as the teacher in my Nursery School. The other one is called Golden Rain and she has long yellow hair and a big tummy with a baby in it that's going to come out shortly. She says it will come out to play but it won't. It'll be too teenytiny and all outofsorts for that. Shortly means in a little while but not as soon as soon.

When I go to Big School I'm going to make a steam engine all out of bitsandbobs and learn to read and write. I'm nearly ready for Big School because I can touch my ear over my head. I already have piggytails and I have bobbles, yellow bobbles, and I'm old enough to have memries. I haven't got any memries bout being a teenybaby but I do have memries bout being three. I got a present and I was cited cause it was a big present in red paper and Aunty Kathleen said awww she thinks it's Christmas but it was just cause the paper was red and I know bout Christmas and I didn't think that.

Auntie Golde comes back to see if I'm going to stand there all night. At teatime Auntie Golde said that Mummy was marriedout but I don't think that's the same as carriedaway. The grownups say not to get carriedaway when we're all cited but that's what we like and we don't want to stop then and someone doesn't get hurt.

I follow Auntie Golde up the stairs. The stairs go round a corner two times and then it's the top floor where the carpet all runs out and the Box Room is. I don't know if this room is small like a box or for keeping boxes in. There are some boxes in it, big wooden ones with labels on and lots of dust. Daddy says sometimes I really am a gormlessgreateejit, but I know that he's always funning me, cept when I stracted him and he dropped a heavy box on his bare feet. That wasn't funning but I was so scared I laughed anyway. It sounded silly and Daddy was fulloncross that time. I was little then and Ruthie was only a teenybaby.

It's chilly up here where there isn't any more carpet, and Auntie Golde is going up the stairs really fast and pressing BabyDaniel really tight on his nappy. Auntie Golde's legs are everso straight under her woolly skirt. Calves are baby cows but shins aren't anything else. There are hands and feet and legs and eyes but there are other things like thighs and cuticles which I do know bout but I don't always remember whichiswhich. BabyDaniel's face is all wet and red and his spression looks horrorfied but he's bouncing up and down so he can't make any noise cept one that goes up and down with each stair. I can't keep up with them and the blanket gets hooked on the corner of the wall. All I can see is his dangly legs wobbling with each bounce underneath Auntie Golde's elbow. He looks like the puppet that sat on the edge of the stage once, the one that said 'ooh, a egg!' and tried to cross his legs but he couldn't and everyone laughed.

There's a old cot here that I saw once before but I don't know why cause the aunties don't have any babies of their own. At our house his cot is yellow and has picture of a bunnyrabbit on the side. This cot is made of metal. Auntie Golde is so fierce I can't tell if she's cross or not. She puts BabyDaniel in the cot. He doesn't want to lie down but she makes him by squashing him with her hand, and asks me to pass his blanket. There are other baby blankets in there too already, a blue one and a big squishy one that's red and golden. Auntie Golde pushes him inbetween and he starts to suck on the corner of his blanket. He doesn't look sleepy to me. His eyes are stremely openwide and his face is wet.

28

Auntie Golde says, 'now, now, my little prince,' stroking his back. 'And you,' she says, 'can make yourself useful.' He's not everso comfy but she keeps on stroking his back and she sings him a song in a funny language I never heard before. One bit is easy cause the words are just the same ya dada dai all the time, so she makes me join in that part and she sings the bits with words inbetween. I want to ask what the words mean but she hisses at me not to stop singing. It's a nice tune but we sing it hundredsandhundreds of times before he falls asleep.

We sing it so many times that I even know the funny words as well. They come back overandover. Little girls need to help their mamas, Auntie Golde says. While I sing the ya dada dai bit, Auntie Golde whispers me the story. It's bout a man who loves a lady so much that he sings how he'll sell his own boots and sell hankies at the railway station. I never saw anyone sell hankies at the station, but Auntie Golde says he has to do it because this lady is his favourite and he calls her his own little bird and if she doesn't love him he will be like a door without a handle. That would be silly but praps he's a gormlessgreateejit.

It isn't like any of the songs I know. Some of the words have a scrapey noise in them and Auntie Golde is making her voice go round a corner and up and down and all bendy and soft like it never is usually. I want to laugh at her diffrunt voice but I don't. It's a good thing for a girl like me to be able to do, she says, a useful thing, and it will help my poor mother who godknows needs all the help she can get. It makes me very sleepy to sing it and I want to do a big yawn but that would be silly cause I'm not a baby and it isn't bedtime for me.

'Come,' she says, 'soft soft, we go downstairs. The little Prince needs to sleep. Little boys need to grow big and strong.'

'I'm big and strong,' I say.

Auntie Golde makes a sneeze noise and she doesn't say I'm the Eldest even though I am. I'm really cross allofasudden and I want to shout but I might wake him up and he'll cry.

'He's not a Prince,' I say it really quiet to Auntie Golde. 'He's not a Prince, he's a Ruddynuisance.'

VERSIONS OF 'DI SAPOZHKELEKH' ARE AVAILABLE ON YOUTUBE.

Ouenaye at the Post

'THIS IS THE FIRST PUNISHMENT BY BEATING,' THE venerable Patakaspi said, 'that we inflict on any one of our Nation. All must witness this momentous day and know in their hearts what they have seen.'

It was good of the old uncle to say these words for him, for in truth Pinotokaspi himself was quite overcome, whatever he might pretend, so far was he yet blinded in his understanding by the ever pulpish softness of a father's heart. The goose flesh on the little one's arms as the young men bound her wrists with hemp and led her to the post was easily perceived even at some distance. The women had stark refused to do it and now made much show of their scornful looks, though it was needful above all that their eyes should look upon this thing. The menfolk had to this end corralled them within a small enclosure of wattled stakes, made after the fashion of the makeshift fences with which they are used to keep off wild goats from their meagre crops, or occasionally for detaining one of the nanny goats when she is in kid and for her milk thereafter.

Though they are settled now and no longer range like wodwoses all the year, as was once their custom, they never hold their beasts for long, nor travel with them on their wild journeyings and meanders, seeking neither to possess nor by their industry to work up Nature's commodities in any wise above what is at once to their good contentment. This roaming is most profitable in the procuring of furs, and yet, I do maintaine, it is to no purpose that the whole tribe should be conveyed along with the hunting party. The work begun by Father Peaudouce, and continued by my selfe, has, I confesse it, unto the present day met with but little success in this part of the matter.

31

The old man raised his voice louder in similitude of a cracked bell, for there was as yet much murmuring among the people. By tying a withered bundle of twigs to a sapless trunk he had made a switch in likeness to a broom and this he did waggle skywards with his scrawny arm, appearing but little likely as one set up to be a universal reformer and corrector of abuses.

'This is the first cub that we chastise, we that are of the tribe of the bear,' croaked he, yet his voice did grow stronger and I saw he made haste to divert and busy the people with his oratorie.

Since Pinotokaspi has oftentimes in our close converse explained to me how prodigiously is the mother bear admired for her ferocitie and wisdom among them, and the name of the child meaning in their language Skipping Bear, to my mind this topick for his discourses was not marvellous well chosen, and I hoped he might not long ruminate upon this point. Yet was I grateful withall, for Patakaspi was among them an eminent personage, on account of his age and good sense, for they have in their number no chief nor king, but rather are as the descendants of our First Parents who dwelt but in families on the plains, and admire and do reverence to one another only for those various excellencies such as may not be easilie imitated. Thus Pinotokaspi, for all his towardly parts, is venerated most for his curiosity and his artful devising, not for his speed or strength, these being unworthie of remark. For there are here few of the young ones or those in their prime, be they men or women, that cannot run down the nimblest deer by the meer activity of their feet, themselves supplying the part of hounds.

For my selfe, I might have wished it had not been a girl child – though girls be for the most part naughtier, as proceeds from their fleshlie nature; better far a lustie lad more hardened to such usage, all be it such was there never among them neither until that day. This Ouenaye, being of age not above eight or nine years, was much of a bigness with my niece, Thérèse. Some of the men wept openly, streaking the black and ochre upon their faces, and I feared their tender hearts might the more misgive them in such a case – although in truth they testifie not among them as to a difference between their he and she children, the term in their language being 'cubs' for them all; notwithstanding that their youth do go about naked as the

32

new day, that all may see to which designation they belong.

The child's eyes did darken, as she would shew surprize, when Patakaspi explained, with many solemn gestures for the crowd, what must happen to her and the occasion for it. For it yet appeared that she did not apprehend of her own sin – namely, that she did in most wilfull wise disobey her father and her uncle withal and did run abroad when she was express forbid; and, further, that she did answer with most sullen countenance when she was at first called to account and chastised. I did suspect the old rascal, who was, like all his people ever a lover of spectacle, might begin to divine the parts of his occasion most fitful and dramatick, and did nod my head with some sternness that he might not delay. The other children broke out at once in a wailing, to hear that venerable man pronounce as twere the sentence upon their playmate, but the other men at this did somewhat rallie and subdue them to order with their fierce looks.

The children had been placed nearabout the menfolk, with the youngest ones sat all upon a log the length of a split maple before them. I feared the moppet might call upon her father, who did yet but skulke to the side of all this proceeding. The girl's mother being dead of a fever some five years since, might in no wise gainsay or prevent it, yet he, Pinotokaspi, having yielded in the needfulness of the thing, might have strove to make a better shewing thereof. As the girl's offense was against him, so was it more fitting that *he* should do it, and for all that I could not but consider all those hereaboute, how it might the better serve to bear upon their minds to have one such as the elder states man, an eminence among them, enact justice on this foremost occasion.

The old man, his long hair, of iron-grey hue, parted most severe in the middle of his head beneath his diadem of parti-coloured eagle feathers, fell to a-clattering and a-shaking of his quills and bracelets, as I have oft times seen him in this very spot before. Ne'ertheless, I suspected him not of those former sorceries as might have been before the days of Father Peaudouce's most potent diswasions, but rather of subjecting the event in hand to the greatest possible protraction, since he would not by any means permit me to catch his eye, though I sought it most assiduously. Would the wretch never be done? Must he be proclaiming and declaiming all the after-noon?

Yet I own that such tender feelings are but natural in a father, and should be forgiven in an uncle too; in deed it might have touched upon any heart to see her there, how she trembled in the light breeze coming off the river. Howsoever it was, noting she did bite upon her lower lip and would not cry did much serve to remind me that she was a froward wench, and like to be much worse if not early tamed. For women are like bulls and elephants in this respect, as a single glance upon Battelbayou, penned among the other women and making wry mouths until the very moment when the gag was put upon her, must show.

Battelbayou must perforce be of like age with my dear sister, Blanche-Marie, yet here at once all similitude ceases. I did see once a French noblewoman and her party alight at Spanish Port, where were a great number of the people native to the place gathered all together at their baskets in a market. Being a rich and flourishing people, and their furs and other little articles being on all occasions very useful to us, there existed at that time a most perfect tranquillitie and good understanding betwixt us and them, so that the ladies were not in overmuch danger and, in fine, this Comtesse did suffer them to survey her, allowing them to swarm about her wondering and crying out in shews of infinite surprize. For the buttons and silver loops upon her costume were beyond all the little arts and cunning they are capable of and, being arrayed in a taffety cap with feathers and suit of yellow and white with an abundance of pale blue ribbons, she did much provoke their admiration.

I own I was discomfited to see their hands upon her, lifting up her skirts and exclaiming over her petticoats, but this lady being of much courage did not blench, nor stint of discovering for them her shoon, which sight they did receive with great wonder and in especiall the buckles, having always great liking and esteem of all shining things. In fine, she was not one whit frighted but did laugh most heartily at their laying their little hands all about her. Her ladies were in haste to offer the women stockings and garters as gifts, but the young ones who were bold enough to take them put them at once upon their arms, which did occasion much merriment among our French party.

Seeing them rummage so among the many layers of petticoats, I at once perceived that these people could in no wise discern where our dress ended and we began; but in this they are not so foolish neither, for our accoutrements of dress are become and do mark in deed a part of our very selves. For the Lord did command us to cover our selves and instruct us how we might do so. And though my dear Blanche-Marie does prefer greyer hues and is of more modest dress than was this fine lady, when I remembered this little scene I thought no more of Battelbayou and Blanche-Marie.

It was this same Battelbayou who led the women in the great running, that most shameful desertion of all wifely dutie and wholesomeness whatever, a meer sixmonth since. A full seven weeks did they dwell with their children in the forest caverns before the menfolk were able to mount sufficient force and purpose to drag them back againe. This Ouenaye that stood now at the whipping stake must perforce have been among them, with her young cousins, in the monstrous excursion to the caves, whatever her sad eyes might now tell the multitude roundabout of demure looks and dismay. For suchlike little maids are deceiving imps and love-days all, as the whelps of the she-lion, and kittens will soon enough be like to their dam. The women were shut up in their houses a further seven-night, and the ring-leaders put all in a long-house and bound fast. Imprisonment seemed in no measure to have borne upon Battelbayou, for the devil was in her and worked through her, and her husband, poor creature and hapless homunculus that he was, might not hold sway with her even afterwards, for all my prompting and exhortations that he should exert himself and ought to be abashed at his own timorous slothfulness.

It was needful only to regard her insolent eye, to hear her loud tones about the village and her raucous laugh among the women, how she did raise up her palms as she berated her husband or any other man that crossed her, to know her stamp and the stock whence she was engendered. It was needful only to look upon her big smooth belly and her calves and ankles as she beat the dust into a cloud around them, while seeming not to move from the spot yet ever revolving like Satan him selfe. She wore chaines of small beades looped about her heels for the dancing, the musicke which they do make with their very voices assisted by horns and finger bells, rattles, drums and long hollow staves which they do pound upon the earth, and by the noise of which they do keep the cadence of their devilish quadrilles. We have not, in spite of our utmost endeavours, been able to prevent the dancing, which has oft times occasioned all manner of licentious and lewd enjoyments, with the excesses of which the devil him selfe might expect to be fatigued.

* * *

Despite my utmost endeavours, I never could perswade Pinotokaspi as to the undesirabilitie of dancing. I could not but admire his steadfastnesse on this point and he bested me out righte when he did declare that Father Peaudouce did tell them on his first coming among them that the bells and small earthen fires of sweetly smelling brushwood with which the Saskapi dance to welcome the Sun-woman was most like the incense and sanctus bells of our own churches in France. I do recall that the reverend Father did confide that their fable of the sun's daughter, when she did alight among them as the mother of bears, was in the beginning of his dealings with them most conformable, and that a picture he had of the Blessed Virgin haloed in gold did much assist in his illumination of the people.

Suchlike mixter-maxtering was not to be tolerated, but Pinotokaspi's debating with me ever was done in a most reverent sort, and so I did but wagg my finger as at a naughtie boy and with good contentment I set about to purge him of this delusion, seeking above all to distille into his obdurate mind that Christ's Holy Mother was unlike to any other woman soever. For good measure, all be it he gave me lesse concerne for the progress of his soule than did any other of his people, I saw fit to further urge him to regulate his life. For in the matter of our salvation, I took pains to reminde him, notwithstanding that the Lord does initiate, accompanie and complete all things, yet the first steps are in our own power.

This was at my little house, which was builded for Father Peaudouce soon after his coming into the country, of such mud bricks as might be got from the mouth of the river. The tents of the Saskapi are round and cosie, with wooden clefts joining atop them like to

36

a steeple, most solid when digged into the earth and yet easie to move, while their long houses are mounted upon stilts. Pinotokaspi did frequentlie there attend upon me in the winter evenings, at first to aid me in completing my study of their language, long since begun in Grenoble with the aid of Father Peaudouce's most valuable dictionarie, and latterly that I might further instruct him in Scripture, at which exercise he was attentive, and seemed greatly to be affected with it. I never met a man more easie to converse with on divers matters, or to whom it was more pleasing to convey an perpetuall awarenesse of God.

He would lie before my fire like a great hound, always upon the rug which Blanche-Marie had prevailed upon me to bring into the countrie, most like propt upon one elbow or, if the topic did especially rouze him, he would sitt and embrace his knees. The duskie calls from the forest were then of the less frightfull sort and the light from the hearth did catch upon the many intricately carved, encircling rings of polish't bone of his own craftsmanship which did enriche his neck. Oft would he put his head to one side winningly to pay me the better attention, and I would witnesse the vigour creep into his countenance as he did the more completely comprehend what I did say.

Being greatlie famed as a teller of stories he did in his turne imparte how the sun-woman brought the tame moose among them, which because of man's mistake did ever after flee from humane presence, requiring much hunting with arrows. They have likewise an account of a mightie flood, from which the bear escaped on the back of a turtle of immense proportions like to an arke, and a great eagle which didst find again the dry land, like our dove. For the Lord hath revealed som thing of His holy truth, however darkened and cast down by the fiendish machinations of their priests and sorcerours in times past. In the same wise they do have even a tale of a prodigious snake present at the start of the world, though there is in their fables no woman like to our Eve, which was for a time some impediment to Pinotokaspi's comprehensioun. If the Lord spares me, and the mightie work of translating the Scriptures, which was late begun and with which I now proceed, being done, I have it in thought to make a book picturing these beliefs for the enlightening of aftertimes.

I would not have it thought from this that I partake of that fabular belief in a savage nobilitie, like to that by which poets have feigned the Age of Gold or by which we might conceive mankinde in groves of Arcadie or Eden's shrubberie it selfe. Most assuredly, Pinotokaspi is one of my flocke and oughte to have what instruction he mighte at my hands. Though I do well apprehend that the Saskapi doe maintaine themselves in simplicitie and serenitie with little by way of artifice or humane patchwork, and that our endeavour should thus bee to keep them from slaverie and to make them partners in our enterprises, I am not blinded to the devilish nature of their practices. Yet, when I do fear, O Lord, that I have done nothing good in Thy sight, and that I have neither manly fought nor well maintained my battle in Thy name, I do thinke upon my worke with this barbarous man, and trust, albeit without hope, that it may yet weigh in the balance with Thee.

And withall I remain ever indebted to Pinotokaspi as my help meet in the comprehending of their speech, with which I have been able even to enter upon some refinements of Father Peaudouce's great dictionarie. How else might we expecte to unravell the interminable skeins emitting from that far-off Babell Tower by which we are ensnared? Our converse has been ever most usefull and, though attended by all the wild graces, Pinotokaspi causes me oft to marvell at his sufficiencie in point of understanding. The terminations of their tongue, in the pleasing smoothnesse and softnesse of speech, do almost touch upon the Greek. And I have regretted many times that such peoples were not known unto Plato and Aristotle that we might have had the judgement of such mindes as Socrates' upon their case.

I do recall one eventide in speciall when this was borne upon me. It was the end of the summer before this one, and coming presentlie on to darknesse. We did walk together from the edge of the forest, where the air was grown thicke with an infinite swarm of fiery worms as if every twigg had been a burning candle. We were both of us much wearied, he from playing and I from watching of their game of stickball, at which both men and women excell, and the which battles they do conduct over a most wide terrain and many days, catching up the ball of coney skins bestuff't with dried leaves in their nets.

Pinotokaspi did step before me on the path, comely in body, of a civill behaviour and shapely stature, just in dealing and ever courteous to strangers – in this he did comprise the chiefest virtues of the Saskapi. As such, they in no wise compare to the Maraquois, who are an uppish and warlike people, swift to find occasion of offense, and who do but appeare benignant and serviceable, and that onlie at the beginning, as Father Peaudouce did soone uncover. The young men of the Saskapi are in generall much more lively and long-limbed than many weaselly half-grown Frenchmen to be seen in the streets of Paris or Rouen or Grenoble, and but for their sorry custom of striding abroad in summer almost naked – on occasion they do more attend to the dressing of their heads in finery than to covering their privities – they might be mistook for the brave soldiery of any nation whatever.

Att leaste when snow is upon the grounde they do cover them selves with breeches and long cloakes of fur. For winters are in this place of the bitterest cold, all be it for upwards of five months there be a most goodlie temperature, saving that at the end of summer there come diverse great storms and terrible lightnings with much thunder, extreme blasts and contrarie winds, and it is to forestall these that they do oft perform their ceremonies and conjurations.

We were soone glad enough that night to be within doors, and our converse fell upon his people's habit of courting at night when they are in no wise wedded – without proceeding to their other enormities – and to their profligate divorcing at the will or whim of either partie. For among them any he or she may decree their wedd-lock to be ended, and they do oft do so with such exaggerate libertie as can scarce be conceived. In France, I explained to Pinotokaspi most patientlie, women do not rule their husbands. Indeed it is considered great shame, for man is the Master, ordained of God in this matter, and therefore not to be flouted or gainsaid by any she-citizen whatsoever.

'It is not honourable for a woman to love any other man than her husband,' I admonisht him. 'How may you know – this great evill being once among you – that the lad dwelling in your tent is indeed your son and not the seed of another unlawfully implanted?'

It was a great marvel to see how, with the accoutrements of mere animal reason he nonetheless sought to debate with me:

'Ah, Frenchgodman,' he said, for so did he always address me, 'you pale-ones of Great France do love only your own seedlings and yet we are full of softness for all the small ones of our tribe. Did not you tell me that your Great God loves all the cubs of the man-tribe over all the Big World?'

'I must persiste,' said I. 'To whom, then, should you give your tent and your spear, your best hunting knife, when your wife has but committed whoredom in your sight, whatever words may have passed and whatever uncoupling she may have prevailed upon you to believe has been effected between you? For such is the way of woman to unman and bewilder with her pretty reasons. Suchlike practices do effeminate men's minds, are the very corruption of a man's soule, to be cast from him as a menstruous clothe.' He looked confounded and I did not see the need to translate further.

'Yes, yes,' he agreed most suddenly, 'her pretty reasons and her laughing hair; the words of her mouth are many and the kisses likewise.'

I saw he had it, but then he said, 'the wisdom of the mother bear is in the woman and in her childer also, that we may listen to one another and grow always more wise.'

I counselled him that only donkies and fools thought in such a fashion, that it did not become a man to say in this manner – yet he had never seen a donkie, only a mule, and thus our converse was diverted, for as any boy with a shiny pebble or glittering gew-gaw, his mind fell always upon the nearest object which might light his fancy and forgot all that might have broadened his understanding. Still, he was a merrie man and a lightsome, and I fear I did not hold to the subject as well as I might neither, being almost as beguiled by him as by a pretty sweeting of a lad or a girl. With their hairless bodies and white teeth, I own the Saskapi are in truth more nearly alike than men and women are in Europ; and besides the wine was very strong, and since he would not drink the stuff I was required to consume the larger measure my selfe.

Seeing in what horse and mule fashion he did thus mean to

philosophize, I laught out loud and with right good will. Att this, Pinotokaspi did bow his head and his hair, which was of inordinate blacknesse, did falle like a curtaine before his face almost to his breast bone, so that his cheeks and eies were hid. I would not for the worlde that I had given him offense; for the Saskapi do not laugh to show scorne, but only for joy, and sometimes amusement, but Pinotokaspi knew that we did and was the lesse certain whether I did insult him. I assured him that I did not – for I would no more berate a horse or a mule or a child for that which it might not know, so long had almightie Providence seen fit to leave this part of God's kingdom in darknesse. I had told him once before that anger at what is wrong is no sinne, in deede that the very angels did daily gaze upon man's errours and laugh, holding in derision our overweening projectes as soe many Babells, att whiche tyrannick tower the whole populace of heaven did roundlie scoffe. For wrathe and laughter were seated side by side and planted by God in the breast of man for a purgative to follie and an armed guard against every cheate of soules.

Thus I did content my selfe with no further riposte but to commiserate that the men folk should come off so poorly in the battle for the breeches, and did observe that so much chopping and changing must greatlie impede the getting of children through delay of finding new spouses; but he declared that this was not in the leaste the case, and did laugh heartilie him selfe. I owne that in this I was thinking of the futuritie of our new dominions and their utilitie for getting of furs and timber to the universal benefit of our nations, in which the compliancie of the Saskapi and their being in league with us has been most necessarie to the businesse, and their number being already much depleted by the pox coming among them ten years since. I did then at once averre that a people cannot have too many children and was pleased to heare him agree, 'many cubs is good.'

He did then continue that the mothers must be strong and their cubs likewise, and for this they do suckle them at the breast a full four years, and that during this time there come no more children. Father Peaudouce did ever suspect that the women did in some wise bring them off with herbes or other noxious drinkes, though baffled in all his attempts to discover the practice or, worse, that they did bring the babes most privilie and secretlie to birth and sacrifice them to the devil. Battelbayou and divers other crones being the pothecaries it may be supposed he did surmise arighte. The boyling of certain plantes, which are green continuallie in one part of the forest, did of late much serve to diminish the supremacie of the pox, in especiall when those in grippe of the maladie are wont to sit without the tents in fullness of sun-shine, that its heate might draw hence the venomous humours.

Pinotokaspi did draw closer and rise upon his knees as if he would the better instructe me. The Maraquoi, he whispered, do weane their boy childer from their mother's dug with utmost severitie at exactlie two years of age for to make them fearsome warriors. He could not tell me whether this had been ever their practice or proceeded from their late wars with the pale-ones; but the Maraquoi are ever a bye-word in ferocitie, as Father Peaudouce and the seven late so cruelly martyred with him must atteste, whereas the Saskapi are above all a peaceable and serviceable nation for whose utilitie and pliabilitie unto us the Lord be thanked daily.

Wanting to extend our converse, I did addresse him on the shameful refusing of his people ever to beat their children; for this unwarranted leniencie, like the perfidious equitie which they doe allow their women, does make them, as I heard our French commander say when I told him of it, a most unstable partner in our undertakings, and most un-meet for our purposes all together. Pinotokaspi would not agree with me. On the contrarie, he held it for a horrour. I did explaine that such acts of correction cause no surprize in France because it is usuall there to proceed in that manner; but among these people where every one considers him selfe from birth as free as the wild animals that range their great forests it is a marvell – nay rather a miracle – to see a peremptorie command obeyed, or any act of severitie or justice performed.

It is to me ever a wonder to see how even the most bereft of God's creatures do strive after a betterment of their condition and an improvement in their understanding. For, after much pleasant wrangling, Pinotokaspi was that very night at the last prevailed upon to bee my instrument in bringing forth this plan of militancie.

He would, he said speak at first privilie only among the menfolk, not in the publicke forum where the women might occasion strife and foment a veritable porridge of their worthless words on the matter. I had in him the utmost suretie, for the Saskapi set much store by the power of the tongue, in deede in other instances much to the peril of their soules. Their rhetorick doth proceed in a circular fashion and rather work upon he hearer by dint of topicks and phrases oft times repeated to the point of tedium, yet sprinkled with the most surprizing figures or pictures that can be conceived.

They do not, as we do, rely upon trusted authoritie and similitudes but seeke ever the most unexpected comparisons and flowers of speech, such that the hearer is at once wakened from his stupor and must listen close to discover the pointe of all the discours. The Saskapi themselves do most often clap and stamp if a storyteller or speechifier does thus capture their minds, shewing their delight for the most out rageous and fantasticall images that might bee. Pinotokaspi's style is to my judgement rather of an understated varietie, though he is the foremost tale-teller among them and it seems he is the more applauded for his choyce figurative flourishes, as their raritie doth make them the more esteemed.

As I had surmized, his success was very great and his well couch't persuasions did work most effectualie upon the men. How the women most belligerentlie did respond to this new dispensation, running all together into the wooded places, even I did not foresee. Yet the men having decided upon a course did most strenuously prosecute it. In deede this very day it took only the slightest suggestion for them, with a strong and sinewy force of their mindes as well as their bodies, swiftly to constructe the wattle pens.

* * *

I own it was a sight almost melancholie to see, yet the women did remain within this confinement even without the use of tethers, for there were not enough of these manufactured for use upon the goats since, as I said heretofore, the Saskapi kept no such propertie until of late, but instead live by hunting and by trapping the fish which are ever most plentifull. Only the women's mouths were tied, for the preventing of clamouring and endless peals from their quarter, with a reddish cloth, some in the manner of a gag or bridle, stopping their tongue, while others were bound about the chin and jaw with a knot at their ear, which did lend, I confesse, a comical appearance, as if there had been an outbreak of tooth ache among them. When the picture was made of it in wood thereafter the women did appear within the wattle pen all in Roman formation with their gags most neatly tied.

Yet was it needful withall, for it is known that all manner of sorceries and heathenish gagarisms do ever break forth in the utterings of women, even without the promptings of suchlike occasions as this. In deed, did not Pinotokaspi tell me him selfe but last week that the jangling, frothy and immeritous discourse of woman kind did begin overmuch to weary the men of the village on many topicks? I did laugh and told him that such was ever so, and to regard it but as the buzzing of bees or som noxious insecte, and we did discourse upon many weightier matters thereafter, and even I was able to persuade him to take a little of the wine with me.

The beating was not so very bad, at least with respect to severitie – for all his fantasticall gesturings, I do not think Patakaspi went beyond common exertion in such matters – though as to duration, the thing was perhaps a little extended, and I did well discern once againe that the old man had conceived a taste for the theatricks of it all. It was by my reckoning about three of the after-noon. I do not consider that he can have landed upon her above four or five strokes, yet on her back the skin was beat to a whiteness and pink weals did begin to bloom upon it. And now was she fluent in her tears and eloquent in her execrations, for she screamed and sobbed as might any little poppet, and assuredly enough to provide utmost satisfaction to those of us who did witnesse her former recalcitrancie. Such spongey eyes do oft match a supple conscience.

The clouds above the trees being black, and of a heavynesse to signifie that they did carry a deluge that would not long be pent, there came now the distant rollings of the thunder and the first big plashes of rain. This cost me my good repose, and I did begin to feel some anxiousnesse, all be it that it was early for approache of the Season of the Big Rain. I have seen a bough from one of their mightie trees riven from the trunk with such a crack as to herald the end of the world, louder than when the mast of *La Résolution* did topple and the foremost sail was rent end to end on my first coming into Saint Laurence, when I was like to have been shipwrack't and never to have seen this land at all. Ever since I do owne that loud reports and in especiall the rending of canvas does ever induce in me the strongest fearfulnesse of the Almightie and a sore consciousnesse of my own wickednesse.

Patakaspi felt nought ill, and did yet expatiate upon the failure to beat their cubs heretofore, and gather him selfe for, as I perceived, the final blow upon the child. Though the women's mouths were bound, Patakaspi and the other men had commanded that their eyes should be kept open, and the men set to the task endeavoured with pinches to make them do it. Notwithstanding all instruction, many of the women did seek to close their eyes and that indefatigable beast, Battelbayou, and her neerest friend, did somehow contrive to tear off their gags and make of them a blind fold for their eyes in despite of all that might be done to prevent it. But this was not till the last, and by then the torrent was coming on heavier still and the proceeding must needs be halted. The men did lead away the women each by each that they might not consider a great running and desertion as they did before. Yet it seemed that none was so minded and all went meekly enough to their own dwellings.

Ouenaye they did convey to the tent of her grand dam, the women not being permitted to congregate to bathe her for fear of much subversion. With what wondrous forethought they had managed the whole affair can only be marvelled at, for they are a people of much acuity. To pass her into the care of her uncle would have been a crueltie beyond harshness, and so was chosen for the office her oldest boy cousin, that Ouenaye might not too soon reconcile with her father, lest he afford her comfort to the detriment of her instruction. I saw, though, from his eyes when he looked at me from his place by the long hut that tears had much streakt the dust and sootish paint that he, like all the rest, had donned to mark the occasion, so that it ran in dirty lines like the whiskers on the face of a greatlie disconsolated cat. For the amitie I bear him, I would not that he deemed this thing was done for my sake but for his own selfe and the good of them all hereafter. It seemed that he did so

45

regard it, and that he did much wrangle with him selfe such that his satisfaction on this day might match my own. For the pains of one's own flesh must be borne and the terrours of the soul withstood. The way is not without hardship, and tribulations are many upon the road.

The women being gone, the older children were set to cleaning up such little gore as might adhere to the post and to sweeping the dust and the few dropped feathers round about, those that were not trampled. Seeing no cause for further tarrying, I made haste to return to my own little house, finding my shoon much clagged and my cassock all bemired with the commingled rain and dust. I did forbeare to touch the wine by my selfe but did offer up prayers to St Ignatius and to my patron of Grenoble, as well as for the soul of Father Peaudouce, and went swift to my bed for the fire was gone out. The next day, uprysing with no sign of the head ache, I did ensure that one of the other men – though in no wise so fine a workman as Pinotokaspi – did make an engravure for a woodcut of the scene for a keepsake, and for the future instruction and betterment of the people, the which was in aftertimes much marvelled at.

Half-Mast

THE PARENTS HAD GONE TO SPEAK TO THE neighbours about sewerage arrangements, on which Mrs Corby appeared vague. Gone off down the lane, taking two children. The place was almost derelict, they had earlier said, as they drove the mud-spattered mini over the flints of the lane. It would need a lot doing.

The child stood among the cypress trees, letting them breathe for her, the cracked path and Japanese anemones in grey-pink motion between her and the failing porch. No one noticed that she had remained, even Mrs Corby lingering oddly before the house as though uncertain which steps to take.

It was late afternoon, a strange November day, the light moth-veined, like moonrise, in a purple sky. The girl gazed beyond the house to the splayed damson trees, the mound where a wave of ivy swept up over a fallen fence, the hedge brambles sprawling in rusty coils on old rockery stones. They would leave the council house in the large town, with its white kitchen cupboards, its strip of grass beside concrete strewn with tricycles, to come here.

This was the first time they had all been together to see the house. It was hoped that the sale would be concluded today – even though the nephew had not turned up after all – and indeed it had been, drinking tea with Mrs Corby from cups as cracked and stained as the sky was now, waiting in the stone kitchen for the kettle to boil.

The lady being out of the room, the father hoped that the poor old dear's expectations of her nephew were well-founded. She'd be in an old folks' home by Christmas, *he* reckoned.

'Michael!'

'Well, next Christmas then.' Though *they'd* to be grateful, he said, for he did not believe she'd ever have sold up otherwise.

'It's an ill wind,' the mother agreed, seeking to grow comfortable with this idea by resorting to uncharacteristic proverbial wisdom, and drawing her mouth into a wide droop like a frog's. Mrs Corby set great store by her relations, it appeared, and the house, of Victorian brick and faintly eccentric design, occasioned much reference to 'my father the Captain' who built it.

During their tour of the house, the parents had directed their children to the points of interest, with suitable historical explanation: the pump, the former bell-board in the kitchen, fireplaces everywhere 'before people had central heating', the marble-topped washstand in the old lady's bedroom. The wallpaper there was dried forget-me-not blue dusted with small flowers. The eldest girl had stared for a long time, the first to claim her among so many strange things. This pattern, this hue, these pallid sprigs had been arrived at long before she was born. They breathed an older air, spoke of a world unknown to, preceding her.

'Come here, child,' Mrs Corby said, beckoning where she stood. The girl, startled amid the dark cypress trunks, edged forward, socks rubbing together. Mrs Corby did not wait but turned to one side of the house for the child to follow.

Fish lay entranced on the black waters of the pond, like orange rhododendron leaves, eyes upward among the twigs and dead leaves. Perhaps others glimmered below the oily surface, and the two stopped to peer down.

'Take to it kindly,' the old lady said, not looking at her companion but rubbing the backs of her own hands as if she found them sticky. 'It is as it is'.

The child had no inkling what to say. It did not seem to matter. Mrs Corby spoke either to no one, or as if the girl *had* replied. Still the little girl felt as she did when crouched in a hiding place, in those moments before the seeker comes looking. Ninety-nine, a hundred!

Mrs Corby's hat, a species of panama, appeared to have dropped from a great height onto her rose-grey hair, and be about at any moment to re-ascend. This was in contrast to all else about her, which gestured *down*: stockings the colour of weak coffee nagged at her calves above socks and slippers of bulging corduroy. Her flowered overall was somehow battened over the blue skirt and beige sweater which protruded from it.

'That is where my father used to raise the flag each morning.' She flapped an arm towards the hedge, where nettles rose behind a clump of honesty, dangling paper moons.

They might have grown from the old sea charts the Captain had buried there, the child thought, as the toffee tree grew from the wrappers in a story she had read.

They had come to the back of the house, tangling with golden rod gone peppery brown and the charred-looking currant bushes to make a way through.

'My father found many things ugly, and in the end I could not agree. He felt something was being concealed. I was a great disappointment to him,' she spoke as though assenting to something the child had said. 'My father built this place but he did not possess it. He could not understand that. He was not permitted to construct the house as a ship – he wanted more than just the one porthole you know – but he always thought of it as a ship, as something he *steered* in an element opposed to him.

'Will is such a heavy thing in most people,' she observed. 'I saw it in my father. It wore down his teeth, like a horse's, grey and yellow. Transfiguration on the other hand,' she spoke confidentially, 'transfiguration is light. It is easy. When you see, things change. It is not difficult. There is simply a shift of some kind.'

The child did not know these words. Like all her family she was inclined to be quick and to talk a lot, when she was allowed. At six she knew that to be intelligent one is required to show understanding, to *say*. Her parents liked to encourage use of the dictionary, so it was seldom fruitful to *ask* for meaning. Yet now she tried.

'What is it, that Transifigation?'

It was not clear that Mrs Corby had even heard.

'When the deer come, stepping into the garden, I wait with them. And there are always the birds. I give them bread. I love bread. Bread too is easy.'

The greenhouse had fallen, glass turned inside out, dissolving. You could not imagine it had made a sound, that gently imploded chandelier still with traces of vine.

'The strangest things are most perfect, they happen every day'. The woman held tight to the child's arm, then let it go as though she had forgotten what it was. 'You cannot get away from them, unless you stand quite still and go blind – and why should you want to do that?'

The old lady looked straight at her for the first time. Despite a largely benign appearance, the grip on the wrist, the straggling hair, the too-small eyes, more than one face it seemed, made the child in flickers afraid. Yet the tone was kind. The old woman appeared to mind so much what she was saying. The child sensed that it was after all addressed to her, desired strongly to receive, and yet felt herself suspected now of not being in some way up to the mark.

Pursuing this thought, she was not fully listening.

'... and in any case, all that we have is given,' Mrs Corby was saying. The girl sought to compensate for her inattention:

'You mean you get what you're given – and not to make a fuss?' She *knew* it was wrong as she said it.

'I do not mean that ...,' but Mrs Corby was unencumbered by this association of ideas, or the immediate self-reproach of the child, and the severity of her voice was imagined. She gestured to a stooping apple tree.

'My father hanged himself from that apple tree. I watched him at it, took him all morning.'

The six-year-old stared at the ashy flakes of bark around the knots of the tree.

'I offered to help him, but he did not want it, from me. It was a final insult to him I'm afraid. He would not take my help.'

'To hang himself up?' The child wondered, unwisely aloud, and yet this suggestion seemed to reinstate her in the old lady's esteem.

'No, no, to prevent him, but it was an insult all the same. I should have seen that.

It caused him pain,' she added, addressing the remark to the trunk of a nearer tree.

'Go on, dig,' the old woman advised, seeing the child's eye upon some bare earth at the foot of a mound.

With a stick the girl turned the webby earth. There were small nuggets of white in the loamy soil, bits of plate and green glass, old dog bones, slivers of burnt brick, corners of ink-blue tile.

'Gerald shan't have it, you see,' Mrs Corby broke in. Gerald was the nephew, the girl recalled. 'Father would disapprove of course, the male line and what-have-you. As if Gerald wouldn't sell it to the first ... Do you think I don't know what Gerald will do? He may dispose of *me* as he pleases – I am not such a fool as to think otherwise – but *this* ... No, I go because I choose. So that I may choose. I have done what I can to protect it. It has protected me. You will know, I think, what to do.'

The girl heard these words without listening, as, hearing the last chimes of a clock, you often know how many have gone before. For she was putting her hands more and more into the soil, trailing nets of old root, placing to one side the most beautiful pieces of tile. She thought at last to look at Mrs Corby, but the old woman had gone rapt and fumbling, the light of her face reaching out to touch the bowed shapes of the garden under the dark that trickled down the sky.

'*There* you are,' the mother said. 'We wondered where on earth you'd got to.'

'She's a sly little madam!' the father exclaimed, but without his usual energy, or its usual consequences.

It took no time for them all to be shut tight in the car, the girl's brother and sister squabbling beside her. For once she was not the cause of the trouble. The father had embarked on the pretence of involving them in a decision that had already been taken: 'What did they think of it?' etc. etc., answering the questions himself.

'We'd have to clear out that pond,' the mother at last contributed. 'The fish are all dead, did you see? Maybe we could make a garage there, once we've filled it in. There isn't really anywhere for the car at present.'

So they went on, with the car's engine, putting in the central heating, deciding the location of the oil tank, knocking those two rooms into one. The father was looking forward to getting some sense into that garden. It was a shame, but sooner or later those big windows would have to be replaced, the frames were completely rotten. It would be nice to do it in the same style, from a historical point of view of course, but you couldn't always have what you wanted in life. You couldn't easily get sash windows nowadays, not without having them made and going to a lot of expense.

Starling

LADY MACBETH IS A STRONG FEMALE CHARACTER, SHOWING that
Macbeth is a feminist play. This essay will show how Shakespeare
displays a feminist viewpoint by creating such a powerful woman
who rules over her husband. I sigh. Unsex me here. I put it to the
bottom of the pile, replacing the empty ashtray on top, though there
isn't much of a breeze. Maybe best not to start with that one. The first
essay sets the tone, and I don't want to embark on the enterprise in a
state of exasperation or, worse, feeling the beginnings of a crusade.

It's been a late Spring. This is the first day of real sunshine,
though the air is fresh and cold. I reach out to take another sip of
coffee, wincing at the bitterness of it black. I'm trying to cut out milk
at the moment – I can't even remember why – oh yes, for my throat,
and because lattes, mochas and cappuccinos make up the dubious
diet of frothy, sugary drinks in which I have been indulging lately. I
suspect it's mainly for the austerity of it, one of the myriad ways in
which I endeavour to convince myself I'm taking control of my life,
tinkering at the edges as usual. I leaf through the topmost essays of
the pile, peeking at the next three, all on *Twelfth Night*. That ought to
be a bit lighter going. The sea is glittering and calm, an icy grey-blue,
and the light is bouncing in sparkles off the wet sand. I turn my
face to the sun and shut my eyes, drink the warmth into my skin.
The ice-cream sign outside the adjacent cafe creaks. I take off my
scarf. The wooden slats of my chair are hard under my thighs and
the metal legs scrape on the paving slab as I shoogle round to let the
sun soak into my collarbone. My cheeks burn pleasantly. I look again
at the beach. Is this what sun-kissed means? Sun-smooched more
like. Sun-snogged even. Nice.

I pop a brown sugar-lump in my coffee, then another, which plainly defeats the object, but I can't actually manage to drink it without, and if I don't drink it I'll have a headache in no time – and I need to get these exam essays done. There's no avoiding the depressing circularity of my life. There are far too many to do in one day, however many Americanos I consume. I should have made a start last night to be in with a chance of having them finished in time, instead of watching that documentary. Yet, by the time it was evening, the distraction was just too tempting, to pass those few hours without thinking. Another day got through. I could justifiably go to bed to the comforting fantasies of his return, of coming home to find him waiting in his car outside my house, of running into him in some situation where I could say what I have to say, where it can all be explained, resolved. I justify this on the grounds that it helps me sleep, even though in truth these scenarios take hours of wakefulness to run their course.

Then there are the ones where I'm angry, repay him properly for how massively he has hurt and disrespected me, but also something is redeemed, some kind of meaning assigned. I can say no again, properly this time, from a position of strength, and not end up feeling dumped anyway. I get to do what I have never learned to do in real life, quit while I'm ahead. Or I get to show how magnanimous I am, how transcendent, blaming neither him nor myself, show understanding, empathy even, for his violently disposed wife. And through it I receive the balm of his regard, of his continued desire, despite all the impossibility, and even if we arrive at the same place anyway, it will be on the right terms – my terms.

Sometimes when I wake up it's a minute or two before I remember how things are – how they still are. Often it's dark, and the stars are overhead in a sky that's black in spite of the orange city glow beyond the Zoology Building, and the clouds are threading the moon through the branches of the copper beech. I should get blackout curtains, I tell myself, though I will have been twenty years in that house this autumn and I never have. The inadequate straw blinds don't even unfurl anymore. I've been tinkering at the edges all along.

It took weeks of incomprehension before it finally occurred to me that there were benefits to him of her jealousy, that it might suit him to let Moira think more had actually *happened*, and perhaps in his head it had. After all, we'd had plenty of opportunity. Carl had the only car big enough to fit my keyboard and the P.A., so I invariably travelled with him. All those times driving back from gigs, staring at the lorne sausage in the strip-lit, 2 a.m. service station glare as orange as the beans on the plate, the final encore of *Watermelon Man* still playing on a loop in our heads. In the car park we'd say goodnight to Kenny in his Celtic scarf, Al in his rabbinical hat, before heading for the cars. Kenny, the raconteur, used to play bass with Tommy Smith, and he always got a second wind just at this point. We usually stood in the cold longer than we meant. By the time of the last journey Carl and I made together, things had got so intense, I'd avoided the whole issue by pretending to be asleep for the entire three hours. The only way the same evidence could stack up, it dawns on me at last and quite suddenly, would be for him to tell her the exact opposite of the truth, at least the truth as I understand it, to let her think that it had been *me* hitting on *him*. I realise I don't know him at all.

My stars shine darkly over me all right. I feel drowned and foolish and mad all at once. There'll be no lovers' meeting at this journey's end. Anyone with a shred of sense knows that. I scan the essay. The writing is big and sloping and scrawly, in blue biro. Strangely, though, or at least strangely for this batch of students, the writer has remembered to indent the quotations and they are inscribed in a clearer hand, as though the act of transcription occasioned more care, slowed them down. I told Carl it was not on. I told him he should be talking to his wife about the unhappiness he was turning up at my house, early and late, to discuss with *me*. We agreed we wouldn't meet anywhere we would be alone. At least a table between us at all times, we said. I can't pretend that the fact that we needed such measures wasn't intoxicating. Even if all that had occurred was that our farewell hugs had started to last a bit longer than they should, as if neither could quite let go. Can it really be that he experienced me as some temptress, *luring* him?

'It's just the difference that's exciting,' I told him. 'You on-the-spectrum, engineer-types always like me, because I'm mouthy and

55

arty, and save you the trouble of communicating because I can guess what you think.' Not that Carl didn't enjoy language, bandying words. For months we'd couched all our emails about band arrangements and finances in Baltimore drug slang nicked from *The Wire*.

'We're opposites,' I'd insisted. 'We'd drive each other nuts if we were together, you know that. Within six months you'd be complaining I didn't put the lids on jars properly, squeezed the toothpaste the wrong way.' I might have given it a go if we'd both been single, I told myself, but I was pretty certain what the outcome would be – and the loss of that regard and admiration, the descent into criticism and bickering, the kind he and Moira went in for so publicly, it would've been awful – but in any case we weren't both available, so that was that.

He didn't want all this, he'd said – the getting married, the pooling their resources and building the new house, that was all her.

'If I was "her,"' I'd said, 'I wouldn't like being referred to like that, for starters. If you really feel like this, you should be talking to Moira, not me.'

'I'm fifty years old,' he said glumly, 'and I don't know what I like.'

'Yes you do,' I said. 'You just think that what you can have and what you like are different. Why is that?'

I'd enjoyed the sense of myself as some kind of super-wise, sexy relationship counsellor. I'd even deluded myself that I was doing them some good, while relishing the frisson of knowing fine well that *I* was what he liked. I was certainly paying for that cheap thrill now. Only *I* could manage to be the Whore of Babylon without actually succeeding in getting laid, I thought bitterly. Quite an achievement – though I could beat myself up every which way about the hurt I'd managed to cause, about how I should have handled it differently. What kind of fool could've imagined they could keep everyone happy in that situation, not lose either of them? Moira was on husband number three, and, I suspected privately, so delighted to have her fears of growing old alone allayed that she had embarked on the ageing-in-tandem process straight away, the pair of them forever going on about how very *old* they were.

'You can imagine how much she has invested in this – you're the first half-way reliable man she's been involved with, at least if the other two were the complete jerks you're telling me they were. After twice with philandering losers like that, if you cheat on her too, how can she avoid the idea that it's something about *her*, or at least about the men she chooses? Your job is to be *not* like them, and, with impossible guys like that, she won't have had any practice at resolving stuff – so you really need to give her the chance.'

God, I was good. Perhaps I should have thought a bit more about the men *I* chose. Or even the fact that I tended to let them choose me. I never mistook Carl for a courageous man, but, getting to know him better, I did think I had identified kindness as his salient feature and I had relied on that. 'Only the unkind are deformed', the blue biro shared with me. 'The only blemish is the mind'. I can blame his frailty or my own, but we are made of what we are and I bear my evils alone, as I suppose does he.

Sometimes it requires courage to be kind anyway – and, besides, there would have been a competing claim on his kindness, faced with a distraught, betrayed, enraged wife, the pain that had been so often referred to in the abstract at last palpable, before his eyes. How could he not tell her what she wanted to hear, what anyone in her situation wants to hear? It was *that woman*, she beguiled me. I was a fool, it meant nothing, was just a physical infatuation. Did he come up with that or just concur with the account she offered him? The hurtful thing was the sense that he might have come even to believe it. How was that possible? His final email, the obligatory 'I never want to see you again' missive, was so manifestly composed under Moira's gaze, the misplaced commas punctuating the prose like the blinks in a hostage video:

'I'm now thoroughly ashamed of myself and the pain I have caused the woman I truly love. Please have the grace to leave us alone,' he'd written.

The use of 'grace' was peculiarly offensive. Corrupter of words.

In the long email I wrote but never sent, after it all blew up, I'd even been going to give him permission to blame me – after all, it was him Moira had to stay married to. I was glad I hadn't clicked send – or I'd never have got to know with what alacrity he would do it anyway. Once, he'd said, out of the blue – in retrospect an odd question for someone with whom you *weren't* having an affair

– 'What do you want? Do you want me to leave Moira?' – and my answer had come back – quick as a shot with absolute certainty from my gut – good god, no! So I hadn't chosen him, really. Was he angry, dismayed? He had a life that gave him many of the things he wanted and needed, I pointed out. I liked and respected Moira. I didn't want to be the cause of her suffering. I wonder now whether it was just cowardice on my part.

Why am I even surprised? I think, taking a scoof of cold coffee dregs. Dickishness is everywhere, indiscriminate as sunshine. Of course it meant something – it's disrespectful to her as well as to me to say that it didn't. Unless you can both acknowledge that, you'll be stuck in a big, unexamined lie.

'You are a menace to decent society,' she'd said in her final email. 'Stay away from any of our events. If I see you again I won't be responsible for my actions.'

Righteous rage and abject shame, that'll keep you tied together for a good long time, but what will you learn? I'm doing that thing of talking to them in my head again. I hate that. My lips are managing not to move, but my hands keep trying to make little gestures to go with the imaginary conversation.

And meanwhile there's the oddity of existing, of going on existing, in the same town. They've perfected their little *ostracisme à deux*, always as far away as possible, with their backs turned, on the opposite side of the room in any gathering. Carl pulled out of the band, to the bemusement of Al and Kenny, with little explanation beyond lack of time, leaving them to find a stand-in for all our pre-booked gigs. I couldn't tell them why either. Shame is evidently meant to be catching. Still, my imagination persists, one day I'll run into him, and somehow the opportunity will arise for me to observe:

'It's still there, isn't it? The thing you lie about and deny had any meaning. Of course it had meaning. It wouldn't have been a problem otherwise.'

At some point in the conversation, he'll be so reminded of how I am – because I will of course be completely in command of the situation and handle it with such equanimity and forbearance – that he'll be compelled to blurt out, 'I really miss you, you know.' And I'll have the pleasure of saying: 'And that's supposed to be of interest to me why, exactly?' And he'll reply, as he did once before, 'You know I can't look at you without wanting to kiss you.'

I look at my empty coffee cup and try to breathe slowly so that I don't cry. It is easy to feel the injustice of having to take the rap not just for my own part in all this but for his, and even hers, as well – yet when all's said and done, if I'm innocent as charged then I get off only on a technicality. In all the self-justification, it's important to remember that. I look out at the steady advance of the breakers as the tide comes in, a couple of hopeful surfers bobbing blackly among the surging grey. Surely I wasn't completely deluded in my sense that it was lovely to have a friend – a bit like having an older brother, and I'd never had one of those – someone to tease you, pull your plaits and give you horsey fly pinches but punch anyone else who gave you a hard time. It occurred to me more than once that the problem was not that we might be having tempestuous post-gig sex in hotel rooms somewhere off the M80, but that we were having *fun*, openly, in Carl and Moira's living room, trying out arrangements on their ancient piano, or sat on cushions on the floor surrounded by sheaves of set-lists and the scribbled-on scores that spilled out of his sax case, laughing until we fell sideways.

My first exercise in trusting a man since Simon, I think self-pityingly. Great outcome. Well done, me. It is indeed better to be a witty fool than a foolish wit, as the gently scrawled writing on the page propped against my cup advises. Not the least of this heart-sore feeling lies in the humiliating consciousness of my own glaring stupidity. My first impression of Carl, years before I got to know him other than by sight, when he was just another musician and I was still mostly at home with the kids, was that he was some kind of overgrown boy, always in relationships with notably decisive, slightly older women. Not really an adult. Why didn't I stick to that? Now any weary sigh has his name in it, as if I give away my strength on my breath.

Carl had a sister that died. He told me that the first time we ever had a proper conversation. He didn't know why he was telling me, he said. It wasn't important. His mother had only recently told him, on his last visit South to see her. Ettie's views on the parlous state of the world and the responsibility of the darker races in its downfall didn't bear dwelling on. There were a lot of topics to be avoided. He didn't remember it, of course – he'd have been a toddler when it happened; but it made sense somehow.

'What was her name?'

'I didn't know her. She was just a baby.'

'I know, but what was her name? Did your mother tell you?'

'Yes, it was Christine. Little Christine.'

The sky is busy with its own blueness, with the clouds billowing up behind the harbour wall and beyond the Nigg lighthouse. A big Norwegian trawler, red and white, is nosing its way out between the leading lights. I can see the spray from the wake flung up against the grey stone of the wall. From here, it looks as though the wall is moving, drawn backwards, and the ship is motionless, growing larger, longer, being revealed.

I never write comments on the first couple of essays, just notes and suggested marks on a piece of scrap paper, keeping it provisional. Then I come back and more or less re-mark them, writing up the comments from the previous snippets, plump for a mark after I've done all the others. It's not fair to be dishing out marks until you've got the measure of the overall standard. Maybe I'm simply indecisive, or don't feel comfortable exercising judgement. You get into it, of course, into your stride. Perhaps you become more certain of your right to exercise power just by doing it.

Simon never has this problem, this sense of the arbitrariness of it all, but then Simon is a Professor, while I am still teaching on ever shorter and scarcer temporary, hourly-paid contracts. When I was marking the essays for this course a year ago, I had the post-grad Chaucer and the Medieval French ones to do as well, but now it is University policy to save money by getting rid of such part-time staff and axing courses that rely on them. I still have my various moonlighting jobs, my piano pupils and, until recently and by far the most lucrative, the band with Carl and the boys – Kenny the bass player, Al on drums – roping in Jasmine McKenzie when we needed a singer. Why didn't Moira sing with us? Carl said he didn't think her style was a good fit, a bit too country. Ouch! She seemed absolutely fine to me the only time she stood in, for a wedding at a Deeside country hotel, though there was a lot of acrimony on that occasion because Carl had forgotten to pack her shoes. She did a good line in rage, Moira, even ordinarily. I noticed her hands often shook reaching for her mug of tea. Or was that the first stages of something else?

I'd had the chance to observe them up close rather a lot. Having resolved with Carl never to see one another alone, I'd been forever going round to their place. In retrospect, it must look to Moira like I'd deliberately inveigled myself into their domestic space. Yet it seemed as if Moira felt better when I was around, and he was easier, more like the man she'd fallen for. Except for the times when she seemed miffed and kept out of the way, so that I had to keep saying 'are you sure Moira's OK with me being here?' – 'yes, yes, she's just like that sometimes' – she appeared happy to have me there and that he was being nicer to her. Indeed, she often invited me herself. Did they need me somehow for their relationship to function? That was worrying too. Seeing even more of their regular rows was beyond uncomfortable, the manifest pain beneath the apparent trivia. I felt like a child watching parents fighting.

'Why can't I ever be with a man who *likes* my singing?'

I felt for her, I really did. Why couldn't he be more appreciative? But then, he was ferociously self-critical too, and, even after our most successful performances, he'd be full of remorse about some minor and imperceptible error in his sax solo. There was something deathly about his perfectionism, I told him. How awful to have pleased so many people and not to have enjoyed it himself. A couple of sentences before she'd threatened not to be responsible for her actions if she saw me again, there'd been a mysterious reference to having told Carl to 'deal with' my inappropriately familiar, flirtacious behaviour. *When* had this happened? He'd consistently denied that Moira had an issue with my presence or our friendship. Now I'd have put money on it for a certainty that he'd told her I had a crush on him and he was humouring me.

A young starling hops onto the back of the wooden chair at the table next to mine. For a moment he draws the eyes of the customers, recalls my squinting gaze from the sun and the low streaks of cloud over the sea. For that moment we all admire the bright, polka dot flashes of his breast feathers, the keenness of his masked, prehistoric eye in its narrow strip of black toadskin, the polished fingernail curve of his pointy beak. We, the diners, exchange small glances, the man in the T-shirt and sunglasses with his paper, the couple in cycling shorts, acknowledging this briefest of unities. We marvel together at the perfect strength in the bird's spindly legs as he hops from chair back to chair back, half expecting droplets of iridescent green to fly from his feathers as he pauses to shake his little ruff. It's this sticky-up quality that makes him look so pert – a clown, dishevelled and elegant in equal measure; that and his beady eye, the angle of his head, taking in every sight, each opportunity. The plum-coloured sheen of his throat and the gold-and-green spangles among his feathers gleam with newness. A dandy, unconcerned, he hops from slat to slat of the unoccupied chairs.

I teased Carl about that – his love of those tight trousers encasing his long, thin legs, the bright patterned shirts and all-year-round Christmas jumpers. I teased him about a lot of things, spotting his foibles and his certainties, calling him out. At least to start with he was my imaginary older brother, after all, and perhaps this was the younger sister's license, although the facility itself and my tendency to indulge it probably arose from having grown up with a *younger* brother. For me, it formed a way of being around men who were friends rather than lovers. Some didn't like it – a lad I shared a house with at university had told me that once, and I realised it was true, my relentless levity could be oppressive. When I was growing up, my family used teasing as way of being mean while ostensibly only joking, so the person who took offence at the intended meaning could be accused of taking everything, and worst of all of taking themselves, too seriously. As a child, I hated it, studiously avoided replicating it with my own daughters, but it gave you an eye, that training, and I knew, when allied with appreciation, it made for energy and excitement, banter and flirtation. It had been like that with Carl – for both of us – the mocking a kind of observation, a way of seeing one another more clearly, enjoying one another better.

With each movement of the bird, the light catches the ring of purple at his throat, then the green shimmers on different parts of his neck and head and body, glances off the oily sheen of his wings and tail. The grey claws clench the backs of the chairs. Only at one table has his presence gone unnoticed, the one nearest the cafe window, a family of several adults and two young children barricaded into their corner with all the paraphernalia of car seats and buggies and baby carriers piled with the children's red and yellow jackets and the more expensive kind of navy windcheater, the brand of which, for those who know about such things, is probably instantly recognisable. There are two thirty-something women at the table, one the mother, and a plump and wispy-haired baby in a clip-on high chair. Both women inhabit their current role, that of ministering to children, as the totality of their life. Perhaps the whole family does, but I notice the women, because I remember this phase. Who knows what goes on in their heads? Nothing is to be gleaned from their exterior as to how they feel about their plight, which existential questions they might be pondering or what aspirations they might be harbouring. The father, a tall man with a receding hairline and knee-length shorts, goes backwards and forwards into the cafe garnering things they might need and requesting those items which they have forgotten to ask for. The older man mainly occupies himself with helping the boy to manage his baked beans without waving them off his spoon while the two women focus on the baby. I take him to be the father's father, since his grey tonsure follows an identical pattern but in a more advanced state.

When Natasha headed off last year, and with Micah already in her fourth year at Edinburgh, was I a bad mother not to care, just to feel relief – that they were gone, that they were fine – at not having to do anything for anyone else? I must be devastated, many people told me, Moira included. It was only when I re-homed the guinea pigs, took their hutch out of the little room next to the bathroom and scrubbed it in the back garden ready for Mrs Woods to take away, that the house became really quiet. It would look grand in the school garden, the Primary Sevens would love and cherish them, and the miniature swine could roam free during the daytimes. Job done, yet the absence of those talkative squeaks as I stumbled past, half-asleep to switch on the shower, was eerie. I missed the companionable monastic chunterings of Brothers Patrick and Ignatius in their straw-strewn cell, rising to a crescendo at the sound of my footsteps, ever hopeful of some carrot peelings or a clump of parsley. Now I rarely cooked anything that would have occasioned such spoils. Tesco's Finest moussaka or fish pie foraged from the Metro at the nearby garage for me, if I ate at home at all.

With all this time on my hands, there was really no excuse not to finish that book proposal so I could have a publication under my belt, enabling me to *regularise my position*, as Simon would say, or better still apply for jobs somewhere else, where I'd be treated with more respect. At least Simon didn't know about my latest disaster – he'd have a field day with that.

'You always find some drama, some distraction that prevents you from getting on,' he would no doubt charge me.

Simon was full of solutions, and it was my own inexplicable failure to act on his eminently sensible suggestions that was at fault. That tired feminist narrative just wouldn't wash with him, he said. I wasn't quite sure how a bloke got to tell me what kind of narrative I was allowed to have, but I felt, miserably that he was right. Of course some people might think writing a doctorate and bringing up two kids was an achievement in itself – but that was only possible because he was so helpful, he pointed out, with the kids, with everything. In fact, if I ever got a full-time job in the department here it would be down to him, because he had always made it clear that he could work with me and that we were on good terms, despite the split, and all my ingratitude. He'd encouraged me to do the PhD after all. True enough, my research wasn't in his area but he knew the field overall, the way things worked. It was great that I'd completed so successfully, but I hadn't thought the next stage through. I made things up as I went along.

The starling cares for none of this and alights on the post of the cordon separating this cafe from the next one and cocks its head, assessing the spoils of half-eaten crusts and paper napkins and its chances of getting anywhere near them.

'Just ignore it, Joe,' the mother says, in what strikes me as a studiedly weary voice. The little boy cocks his head at exactly the same angle as the starling, who hops sideways along the cordon rail.

'It's a little starling,' the Auntie says.

'Just take no notice. Take no notice,' the mother counters, and

64

immediately ignores her own advice: 'Shoo!' she says, flapping a hand at it above the dinner plates. The starling hops back onto the post, then onto the back of a chair at the table behind.

Sometimes we see off what we would learn more by looking at, I think, sanctimoniously. I needn't be so judgmental. She's just a mother protecting her young. Right, just as Moira was protecting her property, sorry, husband – both are wrong.

The grandfather bawls at the bird: 'Go away, you little blighter!' and at this the baby cowers and starts to cry, dropping her biscuit.

The bird, sensibly, follows the biscuit.

'Go way. Go way, biter – shoo shoo shoo!' shouts Joe, batting at the starling as it makes off with its prize, flutters back to its post. The salt cellar and several cups go flying.

'I told you to *take no notice!*' the mother cries, exasperated. 'That's very naughty. You're a naughty boy, Joe.'

I hate the way adults set kids up, an abuse of power so habitual that they wouldn't even recognise it if it were pointed out to them. All Joe has done is exactly what the two adults showed him was to be done. I wonder briefly whether this infuriates me more than it ought to. Adults set up the game then change the rules, pull rank and catch children out. I'm with the underdog, the unjustly convicted, the kid every time on this one.

The baby is still crying. Joe's flapping has knocked over her tippee cup so she can't now reach it and her biscuit is gone. The Auntie and the mother try to appease her. '*Now* look.

Poor little Baby Olivia.'

The starling has been on the ground hoovering the last of the biscuit crumbs and now flies back to the seat of a nearby chair. Joe squawks and ducks, covering his face with his arms. Getting no response from either of the women, who are busy extracting Baby Olivia from her high chair, Joe shrieks again as the starling hops onto the back of another chair. Diving off his own seat, the boy burrows into his grandfather's side, burying his face as deep as he can in the old man's sweater.

'There,' says Grandad, 'did the nasty bird frighten you?'

It's not children *or* birds, in *Macbeth*, I think. Children *are* birds. Doesn't the wee Macduff boy tell his Ma he'll live as birds do? I fish for the essay at the bottom of the pile. 'The poor wren / The most diminutive of birds, will fight, / Her young ones in the nest, against the owl'. This student writes in black with oddly crossed ts which score out half the word around them. The student has used this quotation alongside the observation that Lady Macduff is a proper mother. I'm momentarily interested to see how the writer is going to square this with his/her conviction that *Macbeth* is a feminist play, but he/she has this covered. A phrase two paragraphs down catches my eye. This demonstrates that women can be powerful and rule over men but sometimes they go too far.

Not for the first time, I wonder whether the students, sweet and well-intentioned though they are, struggle with the idea of fictional representation. For all their evident sophistication, they strike me as oddly literal-minded, and though so techno-savvy, so at home with multiple images and screens and media, they perceive everything as somehow flattened out and simultaneous, equally available in its endless synchronicity. I shift my weight on the hard slats of the chair. All older people think this about the next generation, I realise, and now it has happened to me, for are not my students the age of my children? I feel myself move back a row in the serried ranks stretching into antiquity. I used to have to warn students about making assumptions concerning authorial intention or the existence or relevance of such intention, but nowadays the main problem seemed to be that they saw little need for *interpretation* at all. Tyranny and murder stalk the land, crops fail, birds fly backwards and Scotland goes to Hell in a handcart, but hey, Lady Macbeth is a powerful woman all right.

I think of the documentary I watched last night when I should have been marking. It was about cave painting. I see the big gorge, the viaduct, the broad river and forested bluffs of the valley where the caves were found. I see tiny figures moving about on the pebbled shore, the bison bending down to the quiet water to drink. Once there were as many of them, the beasts and birds, as of us – more, even. Once we saw ourselves among them, a herd among herds, hunters among the hunted and predators among prey, hunters of them and hunted by them in turn; once the odds were in their favour, except for our particular form of ingenuity, a pinch of sheer luck and our endless optimism, with which we painted them in bold clear lines, in the dark lit with our own fires.

All the time, looking at the starling, I've been anthropomorphising like mad, but they didn't do that, the cave people; it was the other way round. Then, we were like *them*, the creatures all around us, and *they* were fearsome and amazing. Once, at a party, I met a young Croatian woman who introduced herself as an auditory archaeologist. She explained that cave paintings occur not in the places in the cave where they would be easiest to execute, or most visually impressive. Not on the smoothest, largest surfaces. No, the vast majority of pre-historic art occurs at the places where the acoustic is the best.

'Really?' I said. 'That's extraordinary. Concert hall acoustic.'

'Well, more or less,' she said.

We didn't look, we sang. Or we didn't just look anyhow. Cave paintings were there not for us to admire our artistry but to sing and stamp and chant our awe and longing and our desire to be like those other creatures, to share their attributes and their power.

I remember a page in my primary school textbook, the cavemen like over-sized boys with seventies sideburns and very bushy haircuts, rushing at woolly mammoths and sabre-toothed tigers with their toy spears and axes, wearing loin cloths and moccasins and ragged furs. The illustration was meant to suggest the inevitability of 'our' rise, the danger and the (largely male) heroism of our early history – the women were all kneeling at fires flipping unleavened pizza on griddles, with babies in papooses on their backs, holding it all together. Yet, this was hindsight, human propaganda. We were just one flock, one pack, among many – the odds were fairer, our hegemony not a foregone conclusion – just a weird and (impressive compensatory sideburns notwithstanding) relatively hairless bunch of creatures, cowering in caves most of the time.

I'm in danger of crying into my coffee. I know that, even though I can see the starling, I'm as far from those ancient people, as far from the bird and the sea and the sky, from my own nature and from the natural in me, as any of Joe's family. I'm angry with them, and I'm angry with Carl and Moira, and with myself for being the oldest kind of fool in the world, but I know the anger is there to be between me and the unending loss of not being chosen; even though I turned

67

him down, even though I didn't choose him. Even though. Behind all this, the grief is big and old and dark as any cave.

At this moment a big, grey people-carrier, a taxi, decides to make a U-turn on the promenade and mounts the pavement right up to the cordon and the plastic base of the ice cream sign, narrowly missing the two bikes chained to the lamp post. For a second it looks as if it will plough into the tables and the wind of its passing causes those seated nearest to sit up. Now *that's* dangerous, I think contemptuously – far more dangerous than a little starling, so smart and scruffy at the same time.

The women at the nearby table are beginning the lengthy task of assembling all the coats and jackets. It's too warm to wear them so they need to find space for them all in the buggy or on the tray underneath it, then to load the baby carrier onto the buggy and balance the car seat, in which the baby presumably arrived, on top, to be taken across the road to the car. The mother has made some attempt at tidying the table, at piling crockery on the napkins so they don't blow away, mopping up the spilled drink and removing various substances from Baby Olivia's face. The father has been inside again, diligently hunter-gathering a clutch of ice-cream cones, which the auntie distributes.

'Is the ice-cream nice, Joe-Joe?' the father asks.

'It's Scottish ice-cream, from one of the islands up North,' his mother tells everyone. She puts the stress on Scottish when she says it, as if the authenticity, the provenance, were a flavour – which for her it probably is. 'Eat it up, then we'll go to the *sand*. You'd like to go to the *sand*, wouldn't you, Joe-Joe?' Again her voice places a strong emphasis on the word 'sand,' almost a reverence. Some features of the natural world have privileged status, evidently. The fantasy of nature co-exists with its utter containment and rejection, I write sententiously in my notebook for no one in particular to read.

I'm great with kids, I suddenly realise. I let them be themselves and don't teach them crap stuff just for the sake of it. My two are grown up now, but I remember this stage, how hard it was, how absorbing, how wearing, how lovely. I don't miss it at all, but I don't think I was ever like this woman, despite all the learning by imitation that goes on. I feel a wave of retrospective self-congratulation.

Joe has fished out his bucket from under the jackets on the tray of the buggy, and the whole party seems ready to move off, but the mother has decided Joe needs another trip to the toilet before they leave, just in case.

'This way, this way,' she ushers him in through the cafe door.

'Why?' says Joe, all ready for his promised foray onto the hallowed sand. '*Why* do I have to? *Why*?'

She doesn't tell him it's because socialisation and compliance with authority, all authority, is required from birth and that the process is well underway in his little life. That's me telling him that, in my head. Even I recognise that this is a bit harsh. The mother knows fine well that Joe will just get down to the water's edge and suddenly want to go, occasioning another huge logistical operation and trek back up to the boulevard. They don't seem like the kind of people to let him pee in a rock pool or consider using the toilets in a cafe of which they have not been customers. Still, she can't see why *why* is the question – why there even needs to be a question.

Maybe something really did get missed out in this process in my own case – not for want of trying on the part of parents and institutions, that's for sure. Maybe I *am* 'a menace to decent society' with 'no regard for social convention,' as Moira wrote in one of her outraged emails. Well, Moira, bite me. I'm a musician and a literary Bohemian, so you've cut me to the quick there! I regret many things in this whole fiasco but my crimes against social convention are not chief among them. I'm not quite sure when, between fending off her husband's only partly wanted advances and trying to make sure no one got hurt, I've exactly transgressed these conventions anyway. 'Marriage is a sacred contract,' she wrote in the same email – the one before she called me a 'sick, twisted, manipulative cunt' and expressed the intention to kill me. Nice language they're using in social work circles these days. I'm not quite sure how the sacred and 'decent society' fit together, but for Moira it seems they're identical. I'm not certain what kind of contract I think marriage is, either, but I was under the impression that it was *voluntary*.

At last Joe reappears and the family begins its stately progress manoeuvring the laden buggy between the tables, the grandfather carrying the overspill and holding the car-seat so it doesn't fall off.

The auntie is pushing, the mother has retrieved Baby Olivia, and Joe is clutching his father's hand with a sticky one of his own and has his bucket in the other, heading for the sea with the slight swagger of a two-year-old's gait, the remaining baby curls at the back of his head lifted by the breeze. As parents, we get so good at pretending to know all the answers we forget we know almost as little as we ever did. It's that pretending until it's real thing again – or until it might as well be. Somewhere along the line we get invested in the adult world, in our own supposed knowledge, our own rectitude. Our unfortunate children accidentally turn us into the very adults who then oppress them.

The young starling is back, perky and tousled as ever. It lands on the empty table, peering with interest at the shiny metal ashtray, which contains the butt of a single roll-up, surveys the landscape of tables, chairs and crockery and incidental human figures with its glittering eye. The woman at the next table gets a picture of it on her phone. A small flock of house sparrows has landed near the bicycles, eyeing the silver bowl of water put out for customers' dogs. The birds array themselves on the spokes, one apiece, as though they're part of some kind of segmented, decorated clock. They take it in turns to bathe in the water-bowl, each time alighting again on their own spoke and inhabiting their own segment once more.

Their furious paddling leaves splashes on the dry pavement. There's been some kind of habitat change, I vaguely recalling hearing on the radio, so sparrows, once so common, have become a rare sight these past few years. The couple on the table nearest the cordon touch each other's arms, drawing each other's attention to a pair of sparrows, who have hopped close to them. The young man extends his phone towards them like an offering, careful to wait for the right focus. The young woman uses her own phone to get a shot of him taking the picture, and they both laugh. Then they try to get a selfie with the sea and clouds as background.

The clouds are greyer now and, though the sun is still bright, small spots of rain begin to fall on the tables. I've scribbled quite a lot in my little book, but the pile of exam scripts remains largely untouched. I can't do this now, and I need to walk – to walk fast and long, into the wind. The fact that it's the kind of rain my own grandad used to call 'wappit,' that seems light but soaks you through in no time, somehow makes this all the more imperative. I gather up my belongings, barely managing to squeeze the wodge of essays into the central section of my cloth tote bag so they won't get drenched, check in my purse to make sure I have enough change for the tip and go inside to pay.

French Leave

LAST NIGHT THE BARN OWL CALLED LIKE A creaking door in the orchard. At dusk I saw it, the great creamy shadow sailing just above the grass-tops between two grizzled plum trees. The mountains glowed. I thought it must rain.

Yet this morning when I woke the sunlight had already settled like a dust on the maize fields and on the mountains – like light on folds of cloth, changing every hour – and on the grey bell-tower of the white church.

Sister Eveline came for me as I was fastening open the shutters in my room. Mother Eveline I should call her now. I was leaning right out marvelling at the outrageous green of the date palm down below – how could anything be that green without being soaking wet? – and recalling the sound of the women's singing from the chapel as we walked in the dark garden, Keir and I, the first night we came.

'It is so beautiful here,' I said to Eveline, still looking out. 'The sunlight washes you pure even before breakfast.' She seemed pleased.

'Come, *chérie*, then we will have this *petit-dejeuner*. Have you slept good?'

'Very well, thank you, except for the owl. It took me ages to work out what it was – it sounded like some spirit come for the unprotected souls.' I made a ghoulish grimace and reached out clutching fingers. She laughed.

'It cannot have any business here then, among such pure ladies. And if he try for sure Sister Katrine will make him change the mind.' We both giggled and Eveline patted my cheek. She was the only person who had ever done that, so when I thought about it, although I knew the feel of it, it was a gesture I could not fully visualise.

'I don't like to think of you all alone in this part of the house. You know you can come into the section of the Sisters. We can give you a room, until he come again.'

'It's very kind of you but I'd rather stay here if you don't mind. It's *our* place, and I don't think the Sisters ... I mean ...'

'Probably you are right. Sister Katrine is more scarey than anything.'

'Oh no, it's Sister Jean Vianney I wouldn't like to meet on a dark night – and there are the ghosts of the dead Sisters to think of too.'

'No, no, my dear, you forget, they are in Heaven.'

'You'd better remind Sister Andrée then. She swore she'd seen poor Mother Bridget on the stairs, *twice*.'

'Ah, Andrée, she is a true daughter of this region. And for sure she loved Mère Brigitte very much. The Mother protected her, and it was her who make it that Andrée has the proper shoes, you know for her foot. I know Andrée feel very alone and without help since Mother Brigitte's accident. I try, but ... it is not enough.' She tugged my sleeve and whispered: 'And I can tell you, I, the new Mother after Mother Brigitte – I, the terrible little woman from Paris who knows nothing how things are done and what is what – I can tell you certainly that Mother Brigitte is not on the stairs, no, she is *everywhere*!' She gave her sanctus-bell laugh. 'Come, I kiss you good morning and we will go down.'

'You always smell so lovely, Eveline,' I told her. Then, pretending to be stern, 'Surely it's not perfume you have on?' When I was a child I used to hide away in one of my dens and put buttercups and speedwells and dog rose petals in water and call it 'perfume.' Eveline's scent was just as I'd always hoped that would be.

'No, no, *chérie* – just a little dab of holy water here and there, it is all we poor nuns are allowed.'

We went out onto the terrace and down the side steps to the kitchen. The part where Keir and I had our rooms had been built on quite recently, in the same pale sandstone as the rest of the convent. We had to have separate rooms of course, given what Eveline had told the Sisters. My *beau-père* indeed – I was a little shocked not just at her invention but at her obvious enjoyment of the lie. No doubt it was highly amusing to watch the nuns, their grimy suspicions usually so far ahead of events, puzzle over us, barely able this time to believe their own dark surmise.

Still, if Keir was my step-father, what did that make Leila, his former wife – a woman who hated me with a passion that would've put Snow White's stepmother to shame? My 'real' mother? What were we supposed to have done with her – left her conveniently somewhere? Killed her off? I don't know why I felt so uncomfortable about this fictional family. After all, I'd renounced family relations in my own case without a qualm. Perhaps that's why, though personally I didn't see why Eveline had to tell them *anything*. We were just here for a month, for a holiday while we thought some things through – where to live, whether Keir could (or indeed wanted to) keep his job. Or why not tell them the truth, instead of letting them guess it in this hole-and-corner way? I mean, if you present people with the truth, or with something that's genuinely good and pure, they always jump one way or the other. It's a kind of test, how they respond, sheep or goats. I find that all the time.

On the small camp-stove in the kitchen Eveline heated up milk, the beads of fat on the surface like sweat on the flanks of a cow. In the bottom of the pan chinked the thick glass disk that stopped the milk from boiling over – a device whose cleverness so delighted me, the epitome of cultural difference, that I thought with amazement of the benighted inhabitants of Britain who had to exist without one. How I loved this kitchen, with its oil-clothed table, its stone sink behind a floral screen, the skitter of lizards on the step, the brown-shuttered window, the date-palm, the mountains. It's so wonderful to wake up in other countries – but here above all. Home countries are like families, they know just how to bring you down.

Eveline gave me a look sideways. I knew what she was doing, checking I was all right, that I was 'taking it' well. It was very kind of her, but there wasn't really anything to 'take'. She's inclined to be anxious about me because when she first knew me, during her posting to England, as she calls it, I was very miserable. I hadn't long left home – I had a boyfriend then, my own age, who treated me very badly. Then Keir came along, and everything fell into place. She really hadn't any call to fret about me now. Surely she knew that.

We drank our bowls of cocoa. I wanted to write him a letter that day – he'd be back long before it could ever reach him, but still I'd have liked to get it down, all my impressions and observations while he'd been away. This week had not been easy, but since Leila had recently moved back to Munich (a place they had both lived some years ago) it seemed natural, with him being just 'next door', so to speak, to go over and see her. Not in most people's book, perhaps – but then Keir and I aren't 'most people'.

'Well, will you come with me this morning – in Charlotte? You can drive her.' I felt suddenly restless. My plan to write the letter didn't seem quite right. I needed to do some more living – Keir would approve of that – collect some more impressions for him to read.

'Yes, yes I'll come,' I decided. I could write the letter after *déjeuner*.

Eveline went for the can of petrol and I steadied it as she poured the contents into Charlotte's tank. Charlotte was a blue, two-seater Ligier with a high trapezoid roof (like the Pope-mobile, we joked), and looked more like a clockwork toy than anything petrol-driven. No licence was needed for this sort of car and they were quite a common sight on the twisty mountain roads, especially popular with teenage sons and daughters working on their parents' farms.

'Have you heard from your *beau-père*?' Eveline asked as I guided Charlotte round a corner screened by tall stems of rose bay willow herb. Red butterflies cavorted on the purple flowers.

'No, he said he'd send a telegram to let me know exactly when he's coming so I can meet the train.' Keir had said originally that he'd be back on Friday, which was yesterday, making his trip exactly a week. 'Leila's a difficult customer you know, and they have things to sort out. I'm not really surprised.' Over the puttering of the car I could hear the stream gushing in the culvert by the roadside. As for the telegram, Keir's always been better at big things than little ones – details really – he's a large-scale person.

Eveline looked at me sideways as if she expected me to say more, which annoyed me. Why should I pour my heart out to her when there wasn't anything to pour?

'What's on your list for this morning, then? What have we got to do exactly?'

'We must prepare the Church in the village, and the one on the mountain, for soon will be the feast of the Virgin and the whole village will make pilgrimage. But this is not so important yet. First we must make ready the village church, for this Sunday we will have again priest. You know,' she winked, 'the priest that *sing*?'

'Oh no, not him.'

'Shh, he is very good man, but his voice is not so good,' she giggled.

I recalled the priest grasping his microphone and rocking from side to side, red with a fury of his own as he led the singing, laying about him with his cracked voice as if he would carry each line to its conclusion by a ferocious act of his own will. Still sweating, and patting his bald head with a cloth, he had delivered a sermon on the evils of the flesh and the particular iniquities of the female – with more than passing reference to the Whore of Babylon, Lot's daughters and Tamar the temple prostitute – to a congregation of two nuns, six black-shawled old women and myself.

'Then I have to see the Mesdames du Plat, the older and the young one, you remember, and poor Jean-Claude, he is home again. We must go to get some of his honey. He make very good honey, like milk, very sweet and full of thickness.'

I was still faintly piqued with Eveline so I didn't really respond. I didn't know why everyone persisted in thinking that Keir going to spend a week or so with his wife was so strange or so problematic. It wasn't problematic to me, for God's sake, so why should they care? I mean, she was his wife, that doesn't just go away. At least, it may with some people, but can't they see that Keir's soul is expansive enough to encompass that? Of course they still have a relationship – and to the small-minded that can mean only one thing. Leila is an extremely manipulative person – I've seen her in action – but he *knows* that. If others hadn't kept insinuating I don't think the question of his being 'unfaithful' (ridiculous term!) would even have *occurred* to me. I know how he feels about me – there's just no contest.

That's when I realised what petty clichés some people are really working with. It was a shock, I must say. I know several friends have thought it strange that I 'let him' go and see Leila at all – no, I'm supposed to drape myself round his neck in a negligé, smelling of recently consumed boxes of dark chocolate and huskily inquire 'When's the divorce coming through, darling?' That's really the kind of level we're talking about.

I nearly stalled Charlotte trying to see round a huge heap of dry corncobs at the edge of a field where the road bent. A single dun cow nibbled at the outskirts of the pile as though unable to take in such plenty.

Eveline was such a transcendent person, I was surprised she could harbour even the shadow of such commonplace doubts. Perhaps some of the Sisters had been on at her. What were they worried about, that I'd be left on their hands, that Keir had just skipped off? How could Eveline, whose spiritual sense was so fine, and who *knew* him, have any worries on that score? What did she imagine he was going to do? Just not come back? Send me a letter in a week or so saying he'd changed his mind?

Gustave the telegraph boy waved at us from the window of his mother's small shop. His grandmother was *patronne* of the adjoining café with its blue and yellow Ricard signs. We took a turning at the barn whose end-wall served as a war memorial: two dozen small plaques with names and dates, and smudgy purple-brown photos under glass of peak-capped, moustached men with dark-ringed eyes.

Eveline's work in the Church was quickly done. I helped her move a stretch of carpet – *Le Messire de Saleich* read one uncovered slab, died 1667 – and unrolled some more. She repositioned three of the tall iron stands for flowers, asking my opinion – Agnès and Monique would come later with the bouquets – then dived into the vestry. She would not be long. I strolled outside, looking up at the bells in the tower, the cypress trees swimming like dark flames behind.

We rattled downhill to the du Plats'. Jean-Claude would be happy to have me to talk to, Eveline explained, someone from far away. He was a very clever man – he had taught at the school in Nouilly just over the mountain, and even for a time at a boarding school in Saint-Girons.

'But I am worried about him,' Eveline confided. 'He seems at this moment very low – how you say, depress'.'

Jean-Claude showed no sign at all of pleasure in my company – unless you count collaring me during a tour of his beehives and expounding in a tone of morose urgency his theory for making honey according to mathematical principles, and his unique way of organising his hives so as to maximise production by harnessing what he called the political instincts of his bees. He turned his head sharply toward me, his black hair sleeked against his scalp like a seal's. His eyes were sorrowful but with a pedantic gleam, as if he approached his sadness also with a certain scholarly rigour and meant to observe its dictates precisely. The black flecks of stubble on his dark skin mirrored the darker strands of wool in his long, green cardigan, from the pockets of which his hands rarely emerged, only to pop back again like a couple of tree-creepers into a hole in a trunk.

I made my escape and returned before him to Eveline and his mother and grandmother, drinking coffee from cups on lace doilies upstairs.

'Once before, you know,' one of the women was saying 'after Marie-Hélène ...' There was a swift change of subject. Mme du Plat the younger got up to offer me coffee. Eveline was admiring the leather-bound account books.

'Of course Jean-Claude does all that – in his *head*, and he writes up the books so beautifully,' the grandmother turned to me.

'Yes it is indeed a pleasure to have him again at home, indeed a pleasure,' the mother's puffy hands smoothed down her apron.

The elder Mme du Plat was wiry and small – her daughter was twice the size of her, a fact that I irrationally found slightly alarming (after all it wasn't as if this tiny woman had had to give birth to her fully grown). Jean-Claude, I realised, fitted exactly in-between, slightly podgy but of no great stature.

'It is not good for him to live always with young children,' the grandmother leaned forward to me. 'They are playing tricks. Sometimes they are nice and they love him, other times they are very bad. It makes him very miserable. He told me' – she leaned over still further and raised her hand to her face, speaking in a whisper – 'he told me he felt like to die, you know.' She made the shape of a noose with her hand round her own throat and jerked her head to one side. I jumped. It seemed so brutal a gesture, so direct for one who made such a play of discretion and concern. 'No, no it is better for him to be at home. It is not much, especially for one so intelligent as he, but he has his books here and we can look after him, the dear one.'

I had the sense his mother thought Jean-Claude was avoiding the company too long. Sure enough she rose, went to the stairs and called his name with the unassuming quaver of complete authority. I heard his step on the stairs. We were pressed to stay but declined, and were urged instead to return that evening.

'Maman has only to kill the fowl,' the younger Mme du Plat assured us. The grandmother disappeared, perhaps galvanised by mention of the fowl. Surely she wouldn't dispatch it there and then in order to press their suit? Eveline thanked them but insisted we could not come.

'They are too kind, the Mesdames,' she sighed as we climbed into Charlotte. She shook her head. 'Too kind.' Jean-Claude and his mother waved from the top of the steps as Charlotte made a shaky start. The old woman was on a wicker chair beside a table under the lean-to roof of one of the outbuildings, sitting with a large grey chicken in her lap looking up at her like a child being read a story. She too smiled and nodded as we drove away.

'You are hungry I think,' Eveline teased me. It was true. Within a few days of our arrival I found myself attuned to the patterns of the institution, waiting for the meal-time bell that Sister Katrine, her grumpy bulldog face all squashed in towards the centre, would hit with the metal bar that hung at the top of the steps beside it. That the bell should be too high for her was just one more thing in Sister Katrine's life – like having to feed Sister Saint-Luc or stand next to Sister Monique, who had a strong tenor voice, in the chapel. She thought she bore it like a trial. In fact she bore it in her face – which she had the habit of turning on you suddenly when you weren't expecting it like a face in a nightmare – so everyone else had to bear it too.

We were almost late for *déjeuner*. The Sisters were already at the table. The food at the convent was not wonderful, but it was French and there was not quite enough of it – a combination which seemed to fuel my obsession. That and the interest-cum-ordeal of eating with the Sisters.

Sister Andrée was telling me eagerly of the days after the war, when Mother Brigitte first came.

'Oh but we were poor, how we lived – *comme des rats, comme des rats.*'

Sister Agnès, who resembled a comfortable medieval abbess, made sure I had a second helping of soup. Sister Saint-Luc sat opposite me, sucking hers from the spoon Katrine held out. She was over eighty and almost blind, the last of the 'orphans' – from the days when the convent had housed an orphanage whose inmates had progressed from embroidering altar cloths to the novitiate ('almost automatically,' Eveline had whispered to me).

'Your *beau-père* will be missing you,' put in Sister Jean Vianney.

'I'm sure he will. I'm missing him too,' I said, putting my chin up and trying to look everyone in the eye at once.

Eveline quickly involved me in a conversation with Monique about her catechism teaching in the local villages. Monique was younger than the other Sisters and very severe. Keir once said she gave the impression of using ninety percent of her intelligence to keep the other ten percent in check.

'Poor Monique, it is torture for her to be shut away with such old ladies,' Eveline had confided. I knew that appeals for help in how to deal with Monique were a recurrent theme in my friend's prayers.

'Like a family,' Andrée was declaring, 'all together, that is how we managed.'

'Of course,' said Jean Vianney, 'in the days of Mother Brigitte many things were different.'

In my room at last, I no longer felt like writing my letter – I didn't believe in it as an act of communication, simply of self-expression. And what had I to say to him except the things I would say if he walked in the door? I tried to imagine meeting him at the station, my trip on the bus to town, seeing him step out of the carriage and catch sight of me, walk to me with his characteristic step that made the air seem to bounce off him as he came. It bothered me that I didn't know where he was now, that I couldn't picture him in a railway carriage, in France already, still in Germany, in a *kondittorei* somewhere, in a bar talking, in her flat. If I concentrated, I felt I should know – but I didn't.

When we were first together I went through a phase of near-panic at the thought that, being older than me, after thirty years or so he would die and leave me. How would I any longer know how to respond, how to be? How could I live up to what he'd shown me, glean from life myself the significance that emanated so effortlessly from everything I encountered with him?

I couldn't write the letter now. I felt too restless. I set off again for the village, on foot this time, past the stone and half-timbered barn of the nearest farm, an old seed-drill tipped on its shafts, a black and white duck with a red blotch on its beak puddling in the dust of the yard. Gustave hurtled towards me on his scooter as I reached the fork in the road at the steepest part of the climb, too fast to see me or answer my wave. In a screech of bald tyres and pittering of small stones he skewed off down the road that led eventually to the villages in the next valley.

'Nothing for me then,' I caught myself thinking.

In the village I stood and peered at the plaques on the barn wall, studying the features in the photographs, reading the same three or four surnames over and over. I turned suddenly, aware of eyes on my back. An old couple were sitting like two magpies on a low wall. I nodded and smiled at them, mouthed *'bonne journée.'* He was unshaven, face inkspotted with age under his dusty beret. Nonetheless he held himself in a way almost dandyish in his baggy blue trousers and short black jacket. She, on the other hand, appeared toothless and dazed, the headscarf knotted under her chin all that tied her head onto her body, an apron over her greying frock.

He hailed me jovially, for I was *la petite jeune Anglaise* who was staying with the Sisters, was I not? I admitted that I was. I had to concentrate, as his French was colloquial and his accent was very strong.

'I,' he declared, 'am the oldest man of Saleich – *le plus vieil homme,'* he repeated for emphasis.

He was certainly very dapper for the ninety-nine years he claimed, lifting his beret to show his hairless head and giving it a hearty slap. His wife looked far older than he – was she the oldest woman, or indeed the oldest person, in Saleich? Either way, it was clear that her age was not deemed a matter of any consequence. Her husband was evidently quite a character and thought of himself as such, embarking on a string of tales of his adventures which I strained to follow, while his wife turned her hands over and over in her lap and nodded at what he said. Still, once I grasped that my association with the Sisters dictated the common theme – namely the miraculous results of faith in general and of his piety in particular – I was able to get the hang of his narrative pretty well.

He rolled up his shirt to show me the scars where a bull had gored him over at Gounod's farm. They were not silver as expected but smudgy black as if a child had scribbled on him. On one side his stomach and chest looked like they had been sucked down a hole. He re-enacteed the whole scene, taking the parts of the bull, himself and the horrified spectators, as well as the doctor, his mother and relations who gave him up for lost. No one had any hopes for his recovery – he was for death, there was no doubt – but he himself prayed to Saint Peter, his own patron, to Saint Roche and to the Virgin at Valatès, the chapel here on the mountain, and lived. Even in the midst of the bull's frenzied attack he had managed to cry out the Virgin's name:

"*O Vierge de Valatès!*" – like that, and that is why.'

His family were doubly blessed by the Holy Mother, for was not his uncle also one of those spared when the *Toinette* survived the tail-end of the typhoon off the Cape Verde Islands, thanks to the prayers of the entire village? The small wooden ship, a copy of the *Toinette*, hung there in the chapel still – had I not seen it?

He was carried away with his tale, as I was, so I hoped he had not noticed my inadequacy, linguistic and otherwise, in the face of it – barely managing 'how awful' and 'how wonderful' in roughly the right places. Now, though, he paused and seemed to expect something more from me, or perhaps just for breath. I ventured:

'Your family has had truly good fortune,' but he snorted:

'Fortune! It was the Virgin I tell you. And not any old Virgin, either. Ours, here at Valatès.' He flicked a hand in the direction of the trees further up the mountain where the small white chapel was concealed. I thought I had blotted my copybook for he got to his feet, hands in pockets, and ambled off, but he had spotted an acquaintance some distance away in front of the café.

I felt I should speak to his wife, if only not to accept her at his valuation, yet before I knew it she had me firmly by the wrist, rhythmically stroking the back of my hand.

'Don't listen to my husband,' she said, 'they all have long tongues here. They eat too much round cheese, the indigestion makes them talkative and gives them strange fantasies. In my village we always said that about the people of Saleich.'

'Where is your village?' I asked her. She named one about four kilometres away over the nearest range of mountains.

'Oh you would not believe what a family I had, such aunts and cousins, no one had such a family as I. My uncles could work and they could dance better than anyone – everybody knew it – and my aunts, so good-looking and so kind. My mother and my Aunt Matilde, they were noted beauties – several of my cousins took after them. Oh you could be proud belonging to such a family. And my mother, such a fine woman, a better baker than anyone else, and so wise, people were always coming to ask her what to do. I stood in the kitchen when she kissed me and tied on the ribbons to my wedding cap the day he took me... the day... took me *away*... and I... such a family I had...'

She began to cry, spitting the sobs out quietly through her floppy mouth, then to wail, her whole body a conduit for that wail that came out in a thin stream of insupportable sound. I was horrified.

'But didn't you... ?' I began.

Didn't she ever see them again? Was it so far – four kilometres? Of course she didn't, you fool. Or if she did what did it matter? Look at her, *look* at her.

I lifted my hand, clenching hers, and patted the soft skin of her cheek soggy from crying, unsure whether I meant to comfort her or longed for her to comfort me.

I didn't see her husband return but *she* did, using my arm to ease herself from the wall. He didn't come close but said something to her I didn't catch. She shot him a look but let go of my hand and shuffled after him still sobbing, a slight moan with every movement as if she creaked.

84

Perhaps it was not so easy to leave everything behind. Loving, close-knit families must be harder to give up than chilly and accusing ones – there was really no comparison – but even so, might not the tentacles of one's early life curl into the future in unforeseen ways? Of course I had gambled all to follow a very different kind of man. Keir – the very fact that I was drawing such parallels demonstrated my unworthiness of him. Still – I felt the sudden fizz of anger – I'd never have left *him* to fret and wonder like this.

I went back down the mountain. The sunlight was mellowing, had lost its afternoon glare. I saw it soften the leaves of the fig tree by the road and the blond stone of the convent down below.

Eveline came out to meet me.

'There's a telegram. His train is coming in less than one hour. You must go quickly,' she said.

Splash!

WE RETURNED FROM BRAZIL ON THE *ASTORIA* IN late July. It was relatively easy to get a passage now that the war was over. There had been rumours of rogue U-boats operating out of Argentina, but after several months the fears subsided and shipping rose towards its pre-war levels. Even booking at the last minute, Dennis was able to get us a very pleasant berth.

We had lived in that country several years so in many ways the voyage was an opportunity to re-orientate ourselves towards our future life. Less so for my husband, of course. Dennis had always been very much caught up in British or rather European affairs, surrounded by British life, as it were, in his work, at least in the beginning. Though latterly his contacts seemed to have been American or Argentine, and at one time he did a lot of business with a German based in Panama (I can't recall his name, I never met the man) which apparently caused some problems amongst the more fastidious of our compatriots, as Den called them. Anyhow, he'd a great deal to do with the Consulate, particularly in the early days, and to begin with he naturally centred himself in the British business communities of Rio or Sao Paolo, though he considered himself far more outgoing and adventurous than they.

It was partly due to this spirit of my husband's that we moved about so much and lived for long periods in quite small towns away from any European or North American influence or contact in our daily lives. One does make certain concessions, as Dennis would say, to the place one lives. He himself would often have to travel to some remote region to wrangle over some tin mine or something with peoples whose *mores* were altogether different than our own. He would describe to me the bizarre rituals in which he had engaged, the people's peculiar preoccupations and sensitivities while oblivious to many of the considerations *we* should deem important. Den was always hugely entertaining in his traveller's tales, but he was serious too. It was his philosophy, his way of getting things done.

There was no point at all in an unbending attitude, refusing to take these people as they were. You'd get no change out of them that way. He had no illusions, he said, and so never made the mistake of proceeding in negotiations as if with a European. Different standards and procedures altogether would do the trick here. It was a matter of expectations and priorities on both sides, and Dennis certainly regarded this, with his willingness to take risks, as the key to his success.

And he *was* hugely successful in those first years. Of course he had to work for it and was often from home. I was frequently left alone with only Deborah and the servants – the cook, the housemaid, the handyman, and Vasti the nursemaid for company. Deborah, being just a little under four years old at our departure, had never known another life, and soon after boarding the *Astoria* I began to feel that I too had not.

The passengers of the liner were overwhelmingly English – apart from a few Americans and the families of some Argentine businessmen – and the atmosphere was definitely, as I may say, triumphantly British. I thought it must be good for me, help me to get my bearings and so forth. I must say I felt like I'd been in a bit of a dream before. There were ever so many amusements on board, games and so forth, especially for the young people. Dennis made friends at once of course – he has always done so easily – but at first I kept pretty much to myself. I felt tense, waiting, as though this time was even less real than the life before, despite being *now* and having to be dealt with constantly. I was always bracing myself. Had the ship hit an iceberg, even at this time of year, I would not have been surprised.

As I said, there were lots of sports, there were games, bridge and billiards and dances in the evenings. Yet I preferred to stand peering over the bow rail at the soapy wake and wonder how deep the water was beneath it and how far away the land we had left. There were entertainments for the children too, but Deborah was too young to take part in many of them without my company or assistance. To be frank, I found it quite a strain to be with her all day. I didn't really know what to do with her without Vasti there. Den was very good, full of fun and instant ideas, and naturally she adored him, but I could see that she needed more time, more working on, to respond properly. To tell the truth, she wasn't used to him. His bursts of hearty affection intimidated her, she who was used to be so much with women, though God knows Vasti was hardly the shrinking violet type. No, Deborah wouldn't commit herself, even to fun, straight away. She was waiting till she could be sure – whereas Den always liked people who could grasp ideas, however daring or different from the ones they were used to, at once. He had to get busy immediately. So with Deborah he would lose interest, which crushed her rather. Besides, he was busy socialising for both of us, since I was hardly pulling my weight in that department.

So I had her rather on my hands. I have never been maternal. Certainly I never wanted more than one child. Not with all that messy birth business, no thank you. They say you forget, but having been through it once I couldn't knowingly place myself in that position again. I loved Deborah, of course, and used to go down to the Nursery and see her regularly when she was small, but once I had adjusted her hair-ribbon, patted her cheek and called her 'fish-face' there didn't seem to be an awful lot else to do. When Vasti came she somehow freed me because she seemed to have no expectations, or at least I had the sense that whatever I did or did not do with Deborah met them fully. I supposed one shouldn't care about the opinions of one's servants, and certainly no woman of my station would be expected to be much involved in the day to day care of her child.

At any rate, a Nanny would have to be found for Deborah once we got up to Manchester. Despite the difficulties I was experiencing, I can't say I relished the prospect – nor Manchester either, though I hadn't said. It was a prejudice really, after all, for I'd never been there. Clearly, with some aspects of Den's business running into such difficulties in Brazil, it made sense to move where he saw the openings were. I didn't know much about his business dealings, not details anyway, but I kept wondering if we couldn't have stayed, cut our losses in those areas and built up again, but Dennis never liked to retrace his steps. I remember when he courted me up at Box, and we used to go on long rambles past the lilac gardens and almost as far as the Carpenter-Garniers' deer park, he would never go back the way we had come. Even if we came to a dead end or an

impassable place, he would find some way round or through, lifting me into a tree to get over some fence or other when we'd come too close to the water-meadows. I thought it all a great adventure.

Manchester. I wish I could see in that word all the opportunities that Den gets so excited about. I imagine grey streets, drab clothes, bomb damage, rationing, the Labour Government. Surprisingly, this animates Dennis most of all. He dislikes Socialism – he won't be told what to do by anyone, he has to think for himself. No, he's always been against any form of Socialism, though he's no doubt it will eventually take over most places in the world. It's inevitable, he maintains. I still find it hard to imagine him living under a Labour Government, working under them. Won't it be desperately hard, the regulations, and the paperwork? Not to mention the taxes. I've repeated to him all the things I've heard from British friends in Rio.

'It'll be chaos,' he predicts gleefully, 'absolute chaos, El. Think of it. The whole country needs rebuilding. There'll be people who know how to get what they want, how to get things done, looking for new outlets. I've got a friend who can get me in. You've seen his letter. We're made, girl.'

To my further protests he'd simply said:

'Haven't you had enough of this sickening, drowsy country? Well *I* have!'

And he tapped the letter again and swung me round. It seems to me sometimes that Dennis is a person who cannot hold two images, two realities in his head at one time. Brazil was already gone for him, from the moment he got that letter or even before. It was not even the past, a place where we once lived, for it simply did not exist – or perhaps the past did not exist. It was always *now* for him, Manchester, the now of his schemes and plans for it, even while we stood in the dining room at Guajarà with the macaws feeding in the mayuma bushes outside the window and the white, dry light bouncing off the leaves into the room, picking out specks of dust on the polished table.

Whereas I had not had enough, no indeed I had not, though the recent past seemed like a long, heavy-scented dream from which you wake late in the morning, drenched in sweat, as the light pushes between your eyelids, limbs laden with sleep, the pale road to the dark green forest and star-shaped, white flowers that drip like icing from the balcony. There was no connection between that life and this one on the *Astoria,* or between this and the next. My sense of dislocation seemed to take physical form and all my movements were made as if each part of me were in a vice and had to be operated separately. It eased a little as the days went by and I tried to focus on practicalities. I had so little experience of British Nannies. They were rather a censorious bunch, was the impression I had received. They had their own ideas about what was what and were apt to make the less confident or imperious mother feel distinctly uncomfortable. It didn't do to intrude. Several families that we knew in Rio and Sao Paolo, when we lived there briefly that first year, had brought Nannies over with them, though others were happy to make do with the Portuguese girls. We, however, had long moved out to Guajarà by the time Deborah was born. We had Vasti.

She did not come straight away, not for nine or ten months at least. I took a long time to heal after the birth. I felt wretched, which was unusual for me. I've always been up and about, never one to fuss, but I simply couldn't seem to get back on my feet. I could hear the baby wailing as she was walked up and down, up and down, by one of the Portuguese girls from the village that Den had got in to nurse her. It was more a roar, really, than a wail, but with a thin note in it, too, like a seabird. I'd hear that and turn my face to the wall. She had dreadful colic apparently, but I didn't know that. I just thought that was what a baby was, this tiny red mass of screaming, inconsolable flesh.

Dennis was furious. He thought the doctor – he had to get the army one from Cantunama – hadn't made a very good job of it. There'd been forceps, and I lost a lot of blood after, more than I should. I'd been meant to go to Rio, you see, to the Santa Vittoria, but the baby came two weeks earlier than expected, and Den was just back from one of his trips to the South. No, Den was most unimpressed with the doctor-johnnie, said it ought to be looked into, but he soon forgot about it, and I was glad to as well. We were lucky, really. The baby was small but otherwise unharmed. Apart from the colic, which passed in time, she appeared to thrive.

I got up at last, took up my life. Living where we did I could not pay calls or go to parties, or play tennis. When he was home, Dennis would drive me to Cantunama, or to the coast. Otherwise, I wrote letters, and took up the piano again, though I hadn't played for years and the baby grand that was in the house was terribly out of tune – it took two months to get a man up from Ensenada to fix it. I told the nursemaid my plans in the morning if they affected her. I saw the baby after tea. We had a series of girls, all temporary. Deborah was about nine months old. Then Vasti came.

When I think of Vasti I see her walking towards our villa along the white stone track out of the forest, a leather pouch dangling from her long forefinger. This was one of my earliest sights of her, folding back the shutters one morning and stepping out onto the balcony to watch her return from one of her innumerable forays to gather plants. Insects too, I think. She used them for medicines and to make odd drinks for herself. Thankfully she never asked me to try one. Dennis was the one for evil-smelling, native concoctions, not I.

The villa was on a slight rise, and she seemed quite far below me. I was confident she could not see me. Later I would know her better. She had a very striking gait, as if her hips and thighs worked independently of the rest of her, revolving under their own weight, while her feet and the trunk of her body went forward in a straight line. She looked as though she might have walked into that forest hundreds of miles away and simply kept on, without altering a single footfall, until she stepped out of it on the track to our villa.

And that is how I imagine she came to us, though in reality she did not walk into our lives like this at all. Dennis brought her back in the truck from one of his trips. She wasn't the first one – he had brought me other girls before, to help me out he said. Perhaps he meant to stay around for a while, but he soon got called away. There was some trouble at one of the new mines. The local leader was not honouring his agreement. The mine manager and the foreman had done their best.

'After I went to all that trouble,' Den fumed, 'drank that muck of a local wine. Why do I bother?' He was furious but I could tell he was excited too. He loved all this.

Anyhow, he had to go, and it was all sorted out soon enough somehow, for the time being at any rate. I never knew much more about it than that – one simply didn't enquire into one's husband's affairs. Den went and Vasti stayed, assigned to the nursery. Subsequently I had the impression he rather disliked her. Perhaps they had some contretemps early on that I knew nothing about. Certainly Den was never around long enough to take any decision based on this antipathy. Or perhaps he did not dare, since I always had an inkling that he was afraid of her, which amused me greatly – he whom I'd never known daunted by anything.

I suppose to the uninitiated she might have been rather alarming, though I somehow never doubted that many more had found her beautiful. She had very short hair, cropped really. She'd shorn it all off for some purpose I never quite followed and it was just growing back, in tufts rather. She covered it with a red and green head-scarf when she felt like it, but most often not, though she was quite bald when she first came to us. She wore large gold ear-rings and had a gold front tooth. Her mouth was wide and thin like a frog's, and snapped open quick as a clasp on a purse to glitter a smile. I never divined how old she was. She came from some village in the South, but for all her primitive look she had spent several years as a dancer in Rio.

At first, as with the other girls, I had little to do with her. I kept up with my piano practice – all those years of lessons with fussy old Miss Cornwell, and then Mrs Reicher, and yet I was so rusty I might never have learned at all. I don't know whether my technique improved a great deal, but I spent whole days struggling with Schubert or Chopin. They seemed so European and made me think of the streets of grand buildings, the awnings and tramcars and statues in fine squares that Mrs Reicher had sometimes talked of, but I'd seen only on newsreels, and which might, by all accounts, no longer be there. Den was mostly away and of course one feels quite sad on one's own like that – as though the forest has simply sealed one in, like Sleeping Beauty in her castle – and a lot of the sadness went into the playing, so that by the time I finished I didn't feel sad at all but rather reckless and exhilarated.

And one day, feeling like this, so full of restless activity, I crept along the hall to Deborah's playroom and peeped in. She was waiting for Vasti to bring her her milk and sweet biscuit – she was about eighteen months old then and quite bald still. I saw her sitting with her little neck coming so straight out of her shoulders and her head balanced so perkily on the neck, and the dip traced with shadow that ran up the back of her neck, and do you know, I almost felt I should ... I felt something, I don't know ... but what could one do? Ruffle the little hair she had so that it stuck out in a pale fuzz, say a few words to Vasti bringing in the milk, and leave.

Still, I took to making that journey down the hall more often, just to watch unseen, as I thought, at first. Deborah's room was like the inside of a green bottle, the long windows were so overgrown with foliage from the creeper that covered that side of the villa. I would sneak quietly up on the two of them as they squatted on the matting. Vasti would be singing in Portuguese, or in the Indian language she used sometimes, and Deborah, who had been prone to be a rather demanding child, was pacified and would sway and sing likewise. When Deborah was quite a tiny baby, her helplessness so infected and paralysed me that ever afterwards she could reawaken that in me with one look of her tawny eyes. Besides, I felt I had no patience.

Vasti had no patience either, but it did not seem to matter. She simply treated Deborah as if she were a swaddled baby or cloth doll, tossing her about, plumping her down where she wanted her, even when she was three and four years old. She was completely autocratic and her commands were often idiosyncratic, or plain ridiculous I thought – yet Deborah obeyed without a murmur. Maybe she knew that Vasti, once obeyed, might well forget about the task in hand and decide it was time to play, rolling and wrestling on the floor, seeming to invest her full strength in the struggle like an adversary of her own age. Or stalking her about the room, shifting from panther to snake or some other such beast until Deborah was shrieking in real terror.

Of course I flustered in and tried to reprimand Vasti – she wasn't employed to petrify my daughter and so forth. Vasti just laughed, glinting with her tooth, her ear-rings and her eyes, put her head back and yawned, showing pink ridges on the roof of her mouth. When the yawn finished she was still smiling. I was reminded how often her smile, so wickedly quick to come, would hang there longer than you would expect, or think appropriate, as though lingeringly amused at itself. It was certainly disconcerting, and on this occasion infuriating. Den would have set her straight in no time, but Deborah gave me a look somewhere between tedium and dislike and I was nonplussed, unable to continue. She managed Deborah so beautifully, I told myself, I dared not reprimand her.

In fact I was to find that the child herself excelled at this animal becoming, as she called it, though I never mastered it fully, when prevailed on to try. Once, when Deborah and Vasti were showing me Old Spider Monkey and Young Spider Monkey, we all three ended by laughing so much that Deborah fell into my lap and we all rolled over in a heap. Deborah was gasping for breath through her hair looking up at me, and the laughter going on and on. We couldn't stop – it was almost alarming – Vasti's head lolled on my arm, she even bit it, I felt her, the skin just inside the elbow, yet we were still laughing. What crazy times we had. What Den would have thought I don't know. I found afterwards that the stitches at the waist of my housecoat, admittedly rather tight, had all burst apart. I suppose that is what is meant by to split one's sides. Could one split one's actual sides like that I wonder?

Still, I have been running on about Vasti and Deborah and Guajarà when my intention was to speak about the strange incident on board the *Astoria*. There was a young woman on the boat, I did not know her name, it might have been Elizabeth. Libby, perhaps. No one seemed to know her, she was apparently travelling alone, although at first, having seen her several times chatting to a middle-aged lady whom I took to be a relative, I vaguely assumed she must be accompanied by her mother or her aunt. She was only about seventeen or so.

Our daughter Deborah, well I suppose she was rather an angelic little creature if you look at it that way. Very soft, round face, lots of golden curls, that sort of thing, and those tawny eyes that made *me* quite uncomfortable at times but everyone else found quite charming. Well, this girl latched on to Deborah. Could she take her swimming? Could she get her a cake at tea? The girl would take her all over the ship, showing her this and that. Deborah seemed happy enough to go, and I was glad to let her.

She was a little peculiar this girl in her manner, quite oblique, as if her meanings slid sideways out of her words, which themselves followed the sidelong cast of her eyes, which seldom looked at you, and with Deborah she was very intense, always in corners, telling her things. But I thought nothing of it. Probably she was lonely. I felt I didn't like her, but I could hardly complain when she was entertaining my daughter for me by the hour. Normally, God knows, one doesn't object to having one's children taken off one's hands.

I recall one evening there was a Ball. She was dressed very simply in white, with a white circlet round her brow like a flapper. It crossed my mind for moment that she had come in fancy dress. The ship's lights seemed to lend to this band and to the pallor of her face, even to her slightly frizzy brown hair, a sort of green glow like unripe fruit. And I realised with a shock – how could I not have remarked it before? – that from her left shoulder to the hem of her skirt hung a woven plait of gladioli, broad as your hand, creamy white turning to salmon pink at the tips, and at the base of each flower the same unripe green. I don't know why but I thought *how grotesque*, and turned away. Talk about wearing your heart on your sleeve. I couldn't look at those flowers at all, or at her wearing them, the whole evening. Goodness knows where she got hold of them, or how she kept them fresh, preserved them to wear that night, or why, but I really thought it was disgusting to come dressed like that, as if she were flaunting something.

After that I had as little to do with her as I might, but one evening a group of us was sitting drinking after dinner when I sensed her walk behind me. I didn't turn, I still felt *off* her in a way and didn't want to see her. She barely paused behind my chair.

'Your child is crying,' she said, and passed out of the door on the opposite side of the room to that from which she had come.

Naturally I got to my feet and went down to our cabin on the

96

lower deck to see what the matter was. Ever afterwards I have wondered why she drew my attention to Deborah like that. For there was absolutely no sound but for the churning of the engines and people walking about on the deck above my head. Deborah was fast asleep just as I had left her, one knee up, one arm flung out, fingers curled. She hadn't even turned over. Could she have cried out in her sleep perhaps? I felt it rather odd, I must say, but I tucked Deborah up a little more – she always managed to work her feet free of the covers. I could smell her warm face breathing its evening milk. As I ducked to go out of the cabin it came to me quite suddenly that I must not leave her alone for an instant. I must not let her out of my sight. I am not used to such things, nor am I ordinarily very decisive, and the force of this sensation panicked me. I went dashing up the stairs to tell Dennis I would be staying below that evening. There were to be games or something in the billiard room.

'But of course you must come. Don't be so foolish, Eleanor.'

As if to demonstrate that foolishness I could feel myself begin to babble and in my urgency broke off and ran from the room. As I reached the bottom of the flight of steps to the cabin deck, the young woman had Deborah in her arms. She had put her in her blue dressing gown and a pair of that day's white socks, a bit soiled on the soles. One of Deborah's arms was about the girl's neck, and her feet dangled, one higher than the other, like the white flowers on the balcony at home, over the young girl's arm.

'I'm just taking your daughter to the toilet, Mrs Luttrell,' she said.

I pulled Deborah from her arms, ran into the cabin and slammed the door.

She did not try to stop me, though she gave me a look. Her face had the transparent whiteness of the glazed turnips on my plate at dinner, but as to her features, her expression, they remain a blank. People say they will never forget the look on someone's face at such-and-such a moment, yet I am equally sure that I will never recall it. I was acting under a compulsion myself. I could not read hers.

I stood shaking till I nearly dropped Deborah, then I sat down. The poor child was still half-asleep, but beginning to show signs of rousing and perhaps starting to cry. So I laid her down in her bed, just as she was, and smoothed her over, and after a moment I

97

undressed and got in beside her.

The bunk was narrow and not very comfortable, so I could not have expected an easy night. Over and over, in dream after dream, somehow Deborah would slip past me. I was on the deck, at the rail, I would turn away, just for a second, and the corner of my eye would catch her and I'd whip round just as she completed the arc of her fall. I was staring and staring at the place where she had gone under, closed like the neatly sewn seam of a cushion. Then, as if delayed, came the splash.

The dreams took a variety of forms, and started from several different points and situations, but however it began the narrative would end with this echoing splash, the phosphorous lights green on the water. I could see them as though I were actually in the water. Splash! Each time I jerked upright in terror. No doubt I cried out. Then feeling for Deborah, calming a little, dozing, then off again. All night it went on, the gaseous lights of the ship on the water, and, beyond, the sea, black and grey and empty of everything, going on forever.

Just before dawn I dragged myself up, washed my face with cold water and dressed. Dennis had not come to bed. I sat on the bunk facing Deborah and thought of nothing at all.

I huddled her near me as we went up the stairs for breakfast, keeping a sharp eye out for the young woman. There was no sign of her, and by daylight I must say I was feeling rather foolish. The others at breakfast seemed somewhat subdued after their heavy night, and quite a few of our acquaintance were down in their cabins. Dennis went down to change and did not reappear.

To break the awkward silence, I talked rather more than usual. Indeed, it was the first time I had spoken at any length – as I say, I had kept rather to myself in company on this voyage. Since no one else seemed to feel like making conversation I twittered on about my strange sequence of dreams. They looked at me oddly. Didn't I know? That young girl – what was her name? – had thrown herself overboard last night and was drowned. She wasn't missed at first, you see, but later there was quite a commotion. Oh, of course, it must have been after I had gone downstairs.

Well that was a strange thing, wasn't it? Was she afraid to go into that grey-black sea alone? Was the angel-child to keep her company in the cold and lonely wastes of water that wash to the edges of the world? Or was she just seeking comfort in the little girl I wrenched so roughly from her? Could I not have lent my child a while? Was my crude gesture the final insult of a harsh, excluding world? I've often thought about it since. Not that I've really had the time.

Blackbird

WITH GRATITUDE TO MARIE DE FRANCE (C.1170)

SHE PACKED IN HER JOB AT THE POST office. Quite senior she'd been in the finish, but Norman didn't want his wife working when there was no need:

'You stop at home, love, and make things nice.'

So she did stop at home and make things nice. She quite transformed the sitting room. They had a new suite put in and there were fitted units, with daisy-patterned formica, for the kitchen. And of course she didn't expect to be alone for very long, though she wasn't so young now, forty or thereabouts. Still, she seemed to find plenty to do. She was a wise, resourceful, courteous sort of person. Norman had seen that in her, it was part of what he deemed a touch of class. Comely too, with large teeth and brown hair. Joy was her name.

It was to a small pebble-dashed semi that Norman brought her home after the wedding. A quiet registry office do. It was his second after all, and of course her parents wouldn't be coming. Just a few of her girl friends, his sisters, and Keith and Eileen on his side. They would be neighbours when all's said and done, even if they weren't the best example of married bliss themselves. Besides, Keith was Norman's mate, had been for years.

She'd worn a peach suit, had Joy, and a hat that even he considered a bit daft, though it wasn't at all showy. It somehow brought out the shining, almost quivering quality of her face. It made him nervous, too dewy-eyed for his taste, with that little veil. Life wasn't a bed of roses.

It wasn't how she'd looked that day at the Social Club crammed in the corner with the other girls, their smooth tan-nyloned legs all jumbled up and overlapping as they reached for their shandies on the copper-topped table. She'd seemed more refined, more sophisticated than the others. Mind you, she kept herself well, with her neat cuffs and silky blouses, her frosty pink lipstick and well-styled hair. Come to think of it, this hat, too, was quite stylish, with those tiny lilies. Perhaps it was the colour. Or the occasion.

It was odd seeing Keith and Eileen out together for once. Keith and Norman went back a long way, having started in the same month in the same department at British Rail Engineering. When the time came they'd bought not adjoining semis but the two end houses nearest one another, only a gravel driveway and pair of garages between. Not that they ever used the garages: Keith walked to work, while Norman had never lost the habit of parking his car on the street. Like a getaway car, his first wife had once commented in exasperation, having to wheel the pushchair round it to get in her own front gate.

Norman remembered when Keith had married Eileen, a dark, pointy-faced girl, not long after his own first wedding. Now the couple rarely crossed paths, even at home, except for ritualised rows. Eileen drank a bit more than was good for her, it was said, and Keith kept well out of it when he could. Even so, they'd raised three children, more or less, though only one at home now, their afterthought. At least Eileen had resisted the urge to go off with anyone else. More than could be said for Norman's own first wife, who'd upped and off-ed, dragging both kids along with her. It had taken him a long time to get over that, a long time.

Yet he and Keith had stayed friends, he a bachelor again and Keith happy to be out of the road if he could. Though no longer in the same department, they would meet for a drink after work, the two of them or in a group. Among their peers they were well-known and well-respected men, fond of a game of darts and pint of beer, not slow to buy their round or over-keen to hurry home. Sensible and honest men.

Until one day Norman surprised them all and married Joy, carried her off against her parents' will so it was said. Not that anyone had known a thing about it. He'd kept it right quiet. Even Keith didn't get much warning. Still, word gets out and there were jokes in the pub. Some bright spark put 'She's Leaving Home' on the juke-box as Norman walked in and they all had a good laugh. Norman took it well. Perhaps they should have had a honeymoon after all, he reflected, though they'd preferred to spend the money on the house.

Naturally Norman didn't come into The Waggoners as much at first. As for Joy, she'd really made a difference to that place of theirs, the few who saw it in the months after the wedding reported. She had such taste, in a quiet way. And she kept it all beautifully clean. There was a place for everything and everything in its place, from Norman's neatly pressed shirts on the wardrobe shelf to her own knick-knacks precisely arranged on the bureau, the cuff-links and handkerchiefs, the sweet-smelling socks and underwear – a different scent for each compartment, lavender and sandalwood and lemon verbena – right down to her own drawer of fancy scarves. She would pore over these by the hour, laying them side by side, seeing the effect. She thought she would have children but none came.

Perhaps they should see someone about it, a doctor, though she was afraid. Norman seemed not to be concerned, yet she had barely broached the subject with him, she knew, no more than 'Wouldn't it be lovely if we had a kiddie, Norman?' now and then.

'What you want to be doing with all that for? All that muck and racket,' he'd reply easily. He seemed always to be going out the room as he said it, so she couldn't answer him properly. Or once, warming to his theme: 'Wouldn't be much left of your neat tidy house, now you got it so nice. Wouldn't have your rooms just so then, I can tell you, not with kids about. Like a bloody hurricane they are. You'd wear yourself to the bone just cleaning up after them, I can *see you*.'

She took his teasing well, for all she found it quite unkind. Probably she deserved it. She *was* a fusspot with her tidiness. And in truth he *didn't* think she could stand it, she seemed that frail and nervous these days. He'd not noticed it before, during their courtship, seeing her only after work, and once or twice with that family of hers, and, though not in all respects an observant man, more and more she struck him as not quite right.

For one there was the business with the shopping, after she'd gone haring out of Presto's that time in a right old state. Too stuffy in there, probably. At the check-out she'd seemed in a kind of trance. He'd still the sight of her when he thought of it, stood there by the till with her hand out, the girl picking the right coins out of her palm. His own wife stood there like a bloody foreigner as can't manage the money, stood there with her hand out.

Now she never went even to the smaller local shops. He did all that on his way home. Of course, he didn't mind it – he'd been shopping for himself for years – but all the same it wasn't a man's job. He wasn't home while six o'clock most nights, though she did a grand job on the cooking. She was a good cook, always trying out something from them cookery magazines. He'd always to remember to fetch her those. She wrote him up the lists in her clear hand, what to get for the following day, bent over the kitchen table in the mornings, a little apologetically. She made little treats, dainties and such, though he never was much of a one for sweets. He was always that famished when he got in, the main course was the thing, but she always made that very tasty, you couldn't deny.

Norman's ex-wife and the children lived out Dringhouses way, about three miles off, on the other side of town. Relations with Linda were not ideal and he saw the children, a boy and a girl of fourteen and twelve only on odd Saturdays during the school holidays. Usually he went there, or took them somewhere and dropped them back.

Although Joy had extracted as much as she could about Jason and Abigail, it was never hard to tell when Norman didn't want something discussed, and after almost a year of marriage she had yet to meet them. She would have liked him to bring them back one Saturday. Wasn't she their stepmother, after all? Perhaps he thought it would be tricky for them, in their old home, she decided. But as time went on she grew uncertain. Whatever would she say to them? What if they didn't like her? She saw herself through their eyes, advancing over the familiar carpet, her face distorted like a face in a spoon, looming. She had never known any children that age, though the little girl would be easier, surely. She had some pretty things she could give. Abby was dark, wasn't she? She'd have to see her to know what would suit.

As for Norman, he simply did not know how to put those lives together, nor, had he examined it, did he really want to. Though he did not know it he was already ashamed of her. What did *she* know about kids that age? How would she try to entertain them, with her clumsy questions and her fancy cakes? He could already see her in his mind's eye, her face pink and shiny, with her large teeth, leaning towards them frozen on the settee.

After her first tentative questions on the subject, she could not urge him. Even so little strength seemed no longer to be hers. Perhaps it never had been, for all she felt that she had lost it, that she was a failing force. It had been quite different at home, even though to the outside eye she knew she was the prisoner, the dupe of her parents. Yet although her mother and father had confined her, had restricted and gainsaid her in the most crucial areas of her life, although they had contrived to see off her life's opportunities for twenty years, within that confinement she had been unafraid to speak strongly, even harshly. And she knew that they were afraid, that they acknowledged that she had that right as it were owed to her. And though there had for some years seemed no danger of her ever leaving them – so much so that the shock of her sudden departure had genuinely prostrated the mother, for so long an imaginary invalid – the daughter held that ultimate penalty always within her grasp.

Therefore, though she had stayed, she argued, took decisions, was in a way the arbiter of that household. And her parents, such connoisseurs of the differing shades and properties of guilt, and who wielded it as some people paint in oils, not subtly but to instantly recognisable effect, knew that at some level they wronged her – her father in particular sensed it – and were guilty too, savouring it, quaffing their own familiar scent with a kind of enjoyment. And they gave their girl her compensation.

Now she had no such redress. Now this house held her in its pebble-dashed walls. She had made her move. It had taken her twenty years. She had gone where there was to go. There was nowhere else.

Norman felt her withdrawal from him, though in fact she was simply immobile, unable even to pull away. She didn't get out enough. She didn't know anyone round here, though that was her own fault since she never went out. It crossed his mind that Eileen might be a companion for Joy, take her out of herself a bit. Not that he liked Eileen himself, too sharp by half, but a woman might find her different. Perhaps if he had a word with Keith ..... but the chances of Eileen doing anything suggested from that quarter were small. Odd that Joy seemed now so unsociable. He was a sociable man himself and had started going out to the pub again some evenings.

Yet when he first met her she had seemed really one of the girls, had stood out to him among them, but definitely one of them. He liked the way she sat, lively with a sense of humour and a quick eye. Her clothes had never a crease or a speck on them. She took care of herself, you could see that. He liked that in a woman. It was a wonder she had never married and yet because of this she had kept her girlishness. A girl, with a woman's sophistication and insight, her hair always in place and her carefully chosen scent. Now she was still well-groomed but something had dulled. He had hardly known her, not on her own, he hadn't. He should have guessed when he met her family, the father skulking in his shirt-sleeves with the tea-pot, and that mother.

He tried to give it no thought, just let things go on. He went out in the evenings or watched television. She went up to bed to read her paperbacks, or just sat up in the bedroom, sorting. God knows what she found to do up there, the place was spotless as it was. Perhaps she should see someone, a doctor.

'He'd only give me tablets, Norman, make me sleepy,' she said when he mentioned it. 'I'm all right, really I am.'

'We can't have you any *more* dopey now, can we? You're enough in that bed as it is.'

It was said quite kindly. He was glad really that she didn't want to go, and he put an arm awkwardly round her folded elbows. She wanted to respond to the kindness in his tone, but she had grown so distant that by the time it reached her he had stepped back, feeling she shrank from him.

'You're skin and bone, woman,' he said to cover himself. 'Have you got that list, for the morning? Do it now, save you getting up.'

Maybe he wanted her to be really invalid, but she was merely misted over like one of her own ornaments of frosted glass. It wasn't that he minded the shopping so much. All men did that sort of thing when their wives were ill. His own father had done it when his mother was taken bad after her youngest. Of course Sis – his sister Vi – had stepped in and helped out. Done everything for him and the little ones she had, and for a long time after. But Joy, was she ill? What was the matter with her? Perhaps he should get Vi in. His eldest sister had little to do since her husband died.

'It'd be company for you. Sort of keep an eye on you, see you're all right, like.'

With instant cunning Joy scanned her knowledge of Norman's sister. Could Vi be an ally for her? She resolved she could not. Yet in what enterprise did she seek an ally? In the preservation of her own unhappiness which she could barely acknowledge?

'But I *am* all right, Norman, really.'

She began writing out the list. Her writing was very square and regular with beautiful loops and flourishes. She had set much store by her handwriting as a girl. It had been much praised as elegant and unusual when she was younger. She felt it expressed her, a secret code which a man might someday read, as a prince falls in love with a portrait or the knight in a story she once read gazes on drops of blood in the snow. The drops form themselves into the likeness of his lady and he cannot move his eyes from them for many hours. She and the girls at work had always had a good laugh at their own ideas of knights in shining armour. Still, it wasn't really that. Rather the notion that she might be known and loved completely, to the very bottom, that a man might find out completely that for which her hand was the cipher.

If she'd not the sense to go for help, Norman reflected, that was her look-out. And perhaps she really didn't need it. This was just a phase. Well, if she wouldn't see a doctor, he hadn't the time to take her or make her do it. He did not really want to hear the word depression – it was one he didn't like – but at least it was just a state of mind and therefore her own fault in a way. It meant you were not quite right. Preferable at least to that older word, unhappiness, lurking behind, which has causes to be assigned, fingers to point. It was something from her family most like. Good thing he and Joy had no kids. You could give that sort of thing to your kids. He recalled her mother's grey, white-lashed eyes, glaring at him in watery fury on the occasion of their last meeting, the freckles in big ginger patches on the skin around them. Naturally he experienced his wife's strangeness as a rejection of himself. He was not an unkind man, and he had loved her, but she was a dead loss, he concluded, not right in her mind somehow, and he dissociated himself utterly from that.

Perched on the very edge of the bedspread, her knee against the varnished wood of the bureau, she sorted through her drawer of scarves: chiffon, pleated artificial silk, cream and rose and peach, lilac and pale blue. Touching them so softly, holding them up, they seemed to settle like a mist on her fingers. Then her rings, selecting first an amethyst then one with a red stone like a ruby between finger and thumb, plicking them down on the polished surface.

Outside, the pavement lined with sycamores dipped then tilted. The rectangular paving slabs and the row of bare trees began to intersect impossibly in the thick light of winter. The splayed branches of the tree-crowns, like a procession of rake-heads, snagged and ground against one another, blown back against the sky.

* * *

At last it was coming round to Spring. A furry green softness trickled through the branches of the sycamores, though as yet no leaves were there, and the songs of unknown birds were heard in each direction. Joy looked out from the kitchen, and it pleased her that day the flickering of the sun on the glass as she went out into the small conservatory to see to her fuchsias – she had two lovely fuchsias in hanging baskets – her begonias and her Christmas cactus.

The lad from next-door was sometimes about at this hour, with his friends on their bikes after school, though more often he went to theirs to play. Joy loved to watch them tearing up and down the narrow concrete strips leading to the garages, scrunching with their wheels on the gravel as they turned or overshot, or gathering themselves and the whole bike, like a single entity, to spring from the improvised ramps they made. Some days the boy simply mooched about on his own, or with his dog, a long-haired creature of mixed descent but with a large touch of the Old English Sheepdog about him, grey and white with currant eyes peeping through. As for the boy, he had his mother's dark hair, flopping forward like the dog's. His eyes too were dark and an unusual shape, curved underneath and straight on top, almost as if they were upside down, which gave him a curious, exotic look. With his jumper knotted round his waist, his arms were soft and straight about the slightly concave chest. His legs, with their small firm knees, were grey from the day's play, except that he'd an oval white gleam where the inside of his knee-caps rubbed together. As white as snow, the snow of a single night, thought Joy poetically, as she watched him, brisk and valiant on his Chopper bike. She could hardly believe the perfect inner curves of those knees as they flashed past, pedalling like fury. Girls at work had exclaimed over a new baby each time one of them brought theirs in to show:

'Ah, look at him, sleeping so peaceful. He looks that contented. To think we was all like that once. And them little fingers and toes. Isn't he perfect, eh, Joy?'

Now this marvel left her. Not that she had ever fully shared it, being always more afraid that the soft, puffy little red creased thing would howl when it was her turn to hold it, and thus somehow give her away. Babies could *tell,* you know. They knew about inadequacy, about fear. Yet it was not mere miniature scale or perfection that held her now as she gazed at the gaggle of boys on bicycles, but the sheer grubby strength of those limbs, honed by hours of running and clambering, hiding or just scuffing about, completely suited to each gesture and movement that they made. Those lads, even when they simply flopped about in heaps on the grass of the back garden, they fell like their bikes on the gravel, in a single, inevitable motion, one wheel whirring lightly.

She did not know why she should spend so much time reflecting on a group of small boys, or in particular on one small boy, or she might have felt embarrassed. She knew he'd noticed her watching and occasionally sat on the low part of the wall nearest her house while she watered her flowers. Just as it was because she never expected to speak to him that one day she asked him his name.

'Me name's Gareth, but I *'ates* it. So I've swapped wi' t' pup, an now 'e's Gareth an I'm Benjy. Everyone calls me it. 'Cept me Mam.'

She was startled by so many words and the force of his reply. It was so long since she had spoken to anyone.

'It isn't you I heard your school friends call Gaz then?'

She didn't mean to disbelieve him, just said the first thing she thought of, stupid with happiness.

'Well yeah, sometimes they does... Mr Chatband at school, 'e's right funny. Shall I show you 'ow 'e goes when 'e's talkin' to t' class?'

She stood captive in the doorway of the conservatory while the boy hopped on and off the bit of broken down wall where the creosoted fence didn't quite reach, before the garages and strips of concrete and gravel between the two houses. She could stay like that for hours with him sat on the bit of wall, at least nominally, for he was forever bobbing up and jigging about to act out some incident or perform some impersonation.

Some of Benjy's stories were a bit on the tall side, but she knew so little of the world of children and school and television programmes it might all have been true. He did not ask about her, except whether she had been to the seaside. He'd been once. She told him of her trips to Bridlington and, once, to Southport, with the girls from work, and what they'd got up to, but for the most part she listened.

One day he brought to her a battered ukulele with barely a string that he had found:

'I got it up at tip. Me mate tried to chaw it off me but I brayed 'im an' brung it 'ere. See, it plays.'

'Show me,' she said. 'Show me, Benjy.'

And not long after, cupped in his hands, a smallish bird, hurt in the wing. She fetched a box and some old papers.

'Keep it warm. You must keep it warm, Benjy, or the shock will kill it. And give it water. That's more important than food.'

'Oh, I s'll get it up t' me room. Never worry.'

In a day or so the blackbird was hopping about gamely enough. It seemed already quite tame, pecking crumbs from Benjy's hand, balanced on the fence post, dipping and turning as hardy and neat as you please. The boy dug out from somewhere an old rabbit hutch which he lined with newspaper and lodged on the shelf of one of the disused garages, leaving the window ajar. Benjy put out food and water for it in tin lids each evening, and though the bird was to be seen about the back gardens during the day, it seemed to prefer to nest there at night.

Now Joy came gladly out into the garden each morning early, when a soft sun spattered the leaves of the hydrangeas, to hang up the washing and look out across the railway line. She listened for the bird low down beneath the bushes. She thought of the world of it, enclosed in latticed shadows, where all the leaves and stalks are seen from below, the crumbling clods and bits of twigs and last year's leaves. When it fluttered up and began to sing, the notes streamed across her like tiny flecks of light, and in the whole of the world she desired no other place.

* * *

And so the days of summer went, until just after four when he would come to her and perch on the broken wall: Benjy home from school, his school shirt tied by the sleeves about his middle, his dirt-brown arms and paler chest, squatting by the wall or leaping up, while she stood framed by the door frame, one hand raised, unable to move from his face or his words, a prisoner of her own delight.

They ate late, as Norman was always slow coming in. Benjy would be going to bed soon, she thought, as she cooked Norman his tea. At least she liked to think so, for although cries of 'Gareth, Gar*eth*, get here. Get here *now*' had gone out some time ago, she knew they cared little if he actually went to bed, and that he mooched about, watching adult TV or dodging the arguments until well past ten at night.

Nonetheless this *idea* of Benjy's bed-time filled her with such soft longing that, having placed her husband's meal before him, she had to go and stand by the kitchen window, pulling her cardigan round her, smoothing the elbows. The days were shortening. It was already dark, with a misty rain. She tried to peer out at the darkened garden, the washing pole and the railway embankment through the reflection of the kitchen and Norman bent over his meal, the purple-yellow light bulb in its glass shade suspended in the centre of the scene.

111

'What you got to go gawpin' out that window for? Anyone'd think as you were scunnered.'

She did not hear him, or only in retrospect like the chimes of a clock.

'Why don't you put a red light up or something?'

'It's not onto the street,' she said quickly. 'There's no one can see me, Norman.'

After this she really did try. For almost two months she made herself more attentive, making bright, false conversation at first unbearable to her own ears, so that she went early to bed, saying she wanted to read, while Norman watched something downstairs. Yet for the most part Norman was animated and seemed to find her sympathetic, though it was hard for her to concentrate. He appeared to have nothing but complaints: how so and so in the department was a 'moron' – she hated the word – someone else was 'too stupid to live,' and so on.

She could hear the twittering of the television from next-door. Their back door must be open. She never watched the telly herself, unless it was those quiz shows they had on in the early afternoons, the ones where schoolchildren have to join up the squares by answering the questions right. It was amazing how much they knew.

Norman was bawling at her now. What the bloody hell was she doing always standing there?

'It's the birds, Norman,' was all that came to her.

'What birds?' His whole face shortened, condensed with suspicion, but he wasn't yet sure what she was at.

'Blackbird. A blackbird singing.'

'Blackbirds don't sing at this time o' night,' he thundered, more jeeringly than he meant. 'That's nightingales, that is.'

'I've never heard a nightingale,' she said.

'And *I've* never heard a blackbird at eight o'clock of a winter's night. What's the *matter* with you?'

She was sure he would belt her. She screwed up her eyes and hunched her left shoulder ready, steadied herself against the edge of the sink. His chair scraped back with a roar but the bang after that was the door.

She went up to bed, not knowing what else to do. She was unclear how long she slept. There was a noise in the room. Norman was there. He'd found her out all right, he said, coming closer to her upraised in the bed. In his two hands he held the blackbird, pulsing, its eye flickering in panic then for a long moment still. He'd *known* where it was, the horror of that to her.

'Is this the little blighter's been bothering you? He'll not give you any more trouble.'

And he wrung its bloody neck, there before her on the bed. And he threw the corpse onto her so her night-dress was bloodied all down the front, and went away, stamping down the stairs, banging the front door. She didn't scream.

She took a scarf, her finest one, of pale cream silk and enfolded the body. The blood soaked through in two places, a large O and a smaller one that ran together like an eight. She placed it on the broken wall between the two houses, lest Benjy should think her untrue.

When the boy found his bundle she was away up in her room at the front of the house. With the pale scarf he lined a small shell-box she had given him, a seaside gift of long ago. His fingers supported the broken neck, easing the feathers sticky with blood into the confined space, and closed the lid, and kept it by him long after it began to smell.

On the Thursday, Vi came.

Seconds Away

ON SATURDAYS WHEN WE WENT HE WAS WATCHING the wrestling. The grey and violet flicker of TV lit the room. He wouldn't turn the light on now, though the winter afternoons drew in. His chair was right next to the gas fire, and there were orange-brown streaks low down on the white plastic grille where the flame was hottest. The clock, the plastic coffee-mat shaped like a sycamore leaf, the photographs of ourselves years younger and already faded, and one of Mum in school uniform, stood on the shelf over the fire, next to the blue glass octopus we'd brought back from holiday.

'Gurrr, it's a diddle,' he said. 'They 'as it all worked out atween 'em afore'and.'

But I loved to watch, especially the tag-matches. The wiry blond in the cross-over strap costume and impossibly small, laced, lion-tamer boots shot diagonally across the ring and crashed heavily against the ropes. The crowd booed but he bounced upright at once, side-stepping the charge of his opponent. He was meant to be the villain. His brazen attempts to hoodwink the Ref, the way he paused just a second to toss back his bleached locks before diving on or dodging his opponent, infuriated the crowd. His footwork, his gestures, were calculated to suggest extreme deviousness and a certain insupportable fastidiousness. Let others get hurt or dirty rolling around on the floor. *He* wasn't going to. No, you had to want him to lose – him and the dour thuggy one, his team-mate, whose contrasting bulk evoked the mismatched alliances characteristic of evil. The two middling-sized blokes with the relatively unassuming names, like Preston Mike Tomlinson, *they* were the goodies – yet you couldn't but admire the blond one's cheek, his Machiavellian guile.

Still, all his wit could not save him now. Mum went to the kitchen to make sandwiches for our tea. Preston Mike, one knee raised, had him down in a half-Nelson, and there was much grunting and banging on the canvas as he strengthened his hold. The crowd jeered, resisting Blondie's obvious sympathy ploy, as his beating on the floor of the ring took on the intermittent, injured bird's-wing note of despair.

'Gurrr,' roared Grampy, palms well forward on his corduroy knees. "E's a Sooner that one.' His slippers inched along the side of the fender as he pushed his feet further and further in. 'Gwaaan, keep 'im down. Watch 'im. That's a foul that is. Don't let 'im go! Gurrr. Ref's stone blind.'

On Tuesdays after school I went alone. Often he stood me on the cylindrical spin-dryer in the unlighted kitchen, or sat me on the dresser to make me the same height. He tasted of Zubes, which he sucked for his bronchitic chest – it could have been worse, Fisherman's Friends, for instance, to which he resorted on occasion – and there was a kind of white spume on his lips. I kept my mouth closed as far as possible, or as far as was compatible with his tongue being inside, but it was not otherwise unpleasant, simply a rather odd use of my time.

But then, what *isn't* in those years you spend doing nothing in particular but growing up, when where you go and what you do for so many hours of so many days, weeks and years is dictated by others, determined by forces so arbitrary as to seem inevitable? Why else would I be lugging that hefty euphonium case half a mile down a street of bungalow semis every Tuesday for my tea, then a further mile and a half past a Co-op warehouse, an industrial laundry, innumerable houses but no shops, to Band?

Ours being a naval district, the only peripatetic music teacher available at Primary School had been a trumpet player. My teeth were too large and stuck out too far for the trumpet mouthpiece so I played the trombone, since the school possessed one. The Secondary School, however, did not, only a rather dented and discoloured euphonium. Thus, I transferred instrument, and it was in this capacity that I attended Band.

So it all made perfect sense, where I was at that particular moment – for it would have been crazy to take the School Bus home to the village where I lived and be driven back into town again, when Grampy lived just down the road and I could simply carry my euphonium. It was a ridiculous shape, that case. The bell end was heavier, pulling down to front or back, and stuck out, bashing against calves and knees as I walked. I had to keep stopping to change hands or to point the bell the other way, and even so the handle left red cleft-marks on my fingers and palms.

Gudge Heath Lane, that long stretch was called, and the name – with its hints of Trudge and boring dry heathiness – seemed to me to say it all. Paved and urban, with a blackened railway bridge halfway down and a dual carriageway at the bottom, nothing could have less deserved the term 'lane'. There were lanes all about where I lived in the village, and *this* – milking the last dregs of interest from the subject to get my feet another few yards down the road before changing hands *again* – I firmly denied any such status. Even self-pity – and I had lashings of it – could not easily get me down that long road. The physical discomfort and the number of small roads to cross made it impossible to dwell simply in the imagination. Nor were the devices of counting and guessing house numbers, gates or fence posts, paving slabs, lamp-posts or garden gnomes at all effective. I say the houses on that street were innumerable advisedly – and I saved plain counting for emergencies, for really bad days when it poured with rain or I felt ill – for they were simply too many and too tedious for the counter to be able to keep it up. The challenge of overcoming that, even once, wasn't interesting enough either.

Did I enjoy Band? It was not a question I ever asked myself. When I thought of it, I thought of that walk, case crashing against sock tops until I had a bruise – or ought to have had one, I felt. Only secondarily did I picture the activity, the music itself, the pieces I liked – Anchors Aweigh, Sheep May Safely Graze, The Basin Street Blues, we euphoniums warming our mouthpieces under our armpits in some frozen church hall before a performance, or in rehearsal counting with increasing audibility our 12-bars' rest: *one* two three, *two* two three, *three* two three... Yet, somehow, was it seeping into me, this set of experiences, rather than another? Would I, years later,

117

always love a good brass band, heart warm up at the first blast? Would an old lady, decades from now, hum the euphonium part – a good one for once, hardly an oom-pah in sight – to the New World Symphony when it came on the radio?

In the meantime it was a duty, because I had parents who didn't let you *give up* activities once you had *made a commitment.* Had I? So I sat every week, gazing at the backs of the three trombonists in front of me – *fifteen,* they were, the heart-throbs of the band – wondering whether, if I'd still been a trombonist... yet secretly glad to be sitting with the baritones and euphoniums, all younger than me. I felt comfortable with them, having a younger brother and sister. I couldn't have coped with the strain of sitting with the trombonists, three years older older *and* male. I wouldn't have had a clue what to say.

So come Tuesday there I was. Grampy was supposed to give me my tea – he remembered, mostly – a chop, potatoes, and some cabbage which he'd lovingly boil for half an hour. And there was always a jam doughnut and strong brown tea in yellow cups. We ate at the table by the window, peering under the net curtain at the last of the light. Behind us the Virginian urged his horse up some steep and craggy place, dislodging stones, and from the ridge squintingly surveyed the plain beneath the brim of his hat. I would eye the magazine rack under the telephone stand and the black photograph album squashed in behind the Yellow Pages, still there from my last visit. Perhaps he'd let me look at yesterday's *Sun* – I knew today's was too sacred for that – or better still the album. I got him his pills from the sideboard and he counted them out onto the tablecloth: a pink capsule, a small yellow tablet and a large white one.

'You're a good kid, you are,' he'd say. 'You likes your ol' Gramps *you* does.'

He put the pills on the shelf above the fire, next to the sycamore leaf mat, ready to take with his Bovril. He didn't eat much at tea-time himself. Just a couple of biscuits and some cheese with his tea, and a bit of Bovril later.

'Me belly's *gawn* West,' he used to say, plucking at his baggy waistband. 'Feel that,' he'd offer, indicating the line of his stomach, 'straight as pump water.'

I still lingered at the table, half off my chair.

'Come on, Klondyke' he said, sitting down by the fire. 'C'mon over and sit on yer ol' Gramps. I wunt *do* nothin to yer. C'mon, you're a good kid *you* are.'

I saw from the clock that there was three-quarters of an hour before it was time to leave. 'Let's get the album out, Grampy.'

'Gi' yer Grampy a kiss first.'

'Will you get out the album?'

'Course I will, now c'mon over.'

'*All* right.' I breathed the fumy warmth of the gas fire, settled on his knee.

'Gi' us a kiss and lend us a bob.' One arm reached across me and one veiny hand came up to turn my chin.

Yet he *would* get the album, and we'd open out its long black pages sideways on the table between us, where we could get the light on it from the street lamp outside. Once or twice I even talked him into switching on the small lamp on the sideboard.

'Where's me specs? Can't see a *damn* thing.'

We lifted the waxed paper sheets to show the small white-edged squares, neatly pasted in rows, of young women in cloche hats, drop-waisted dresses and pointy shoes, resting bicycles against ivy-covered walls or happy on some outing, young men strolling, hands in pockets or larking outside the pub. It wasn't just the sepia tones, you could see the material of the clothes was different and the long-ago light fell differently on their faces.

Apart from anything else, I was intrigued that anyone could forget as much as Grampy claimed to have done, so many people's names or faces, so many obviously important occasions.

'Quit mammerin' me, will you? You'll 'ave me puggled. What you want to know *that* for?'

'Well, who are these then?'

'Urrr, you're a funny cuts *you* are. That's Glad 'Unt, and that's Jess 'Unt – don't know 'oo that is – 'old on a minute, that's Walter – 'im as they called 'Appy – Lutheridge, an' that's me brother Bert.'

I wrote it all down under each snap. It *must* all be recorded or it would be lost.

'That one? That's Violet Villerboys. What you mean, 'ow d'you

119

spell it? 'Ow d'you think? V-i-l-l-e-b-o-i-s, *Villerboys.* 'Er were a good friend o' yer Gran's.'

His memory for animals, on the other hand, was infallible, luckily for me, eager to know the identity of those two feather-footed horses arching their necks intelligently towards the man between then.

'That's Captain and Bess, that is, with yer Grandad.'

He often seemed to lose a generation, and to speak to me as if I were my mother. 'Harry Biggs,' I corrected sternly, the archivist, insisting on accuracy.

'And that's Nobby, the farm dog, 'im that were a pup from Sam and Jinny up at the *old* farm. That's Jinny there, wi' Nobby. And there's Gran feeding them chickens, and that's 'er, over at Weston I reckon.'

My great-grandmother sat fully clothed in a deckchair on the sand, staring out from under her black hat with a gaze the Virginian would have envied at an absent sea.

'And that's yer Aunt Fanny' – old lady in a stove-pipe hat – 'and yer Aunt Lil and Aunt Daisy, 'er over at Summertown.' These I later discovered were my grandmother's aunts, but even at the time, not knowing this, I had the sensation of time collapsing and ourselves falling backwards into it through the black pages of the album.

Then there was Grampy himself in his various manifestations: in his postman's hat or with an arm round my diminutive Granny, who was wearing his merchant navy uniform, sleeves and bell-bottoms rolled up several times. There he was with shining lips and a full head of hair grinning over his shoulder as he and two other young men in shirtsleeves pushed upright a towering fence post into a squintingly bright, lark-filled, Oxfordshire sky. Then he stood among a group of sailors round a life-belt marked H.M.M.S Gnat. Off the coast North of Shanghai, Grampy explained. The next two photographs featured a kneeling row of men in small hats and pigtails who were being casually beheaded in a square. Unaccountably, to me, they had blindfolds round their heads, not over their eyes. The nearest one looked as though he were talking to himself, one further down the line had his lower lip stuck out in a face my brother still pulled when he cried. Furthest from the camera, you could hardly see the man with the sword, at the moment the shutter clicked bent busily over his work, just a half-raised elbow all there was to show, and, in the dust in front of the line, two heads rolled away from two rumpled bodies as if two straw guys had toppled over, their heads too heavy and not properly secured.

* * *

'And I think it's gonna be a long, long time ... '

I emerged from the darkness and the flashing coloured lights of the Hall into the corridor, its clammy, greenish walls lined with stacked grey plastic chairs.

'I'm not the man they think I am at home, No, no, no, no' was still audible as my friend Mucky came out behind me.

'I'm the Rocket Man,' she sang along. 'I need the bog, you comin?' I shoved the swing doors both at once and they ricocheted against the doorstops as we barged through.

'Changing room bog's nearest, innit?' I said, for the sake of intimacy, knowing full well it was.

'I'm dying for a slash,' Mucky exclaimed, disappearing into a cubicle.

'Hey Kez,' called someone, using her other nickname. Her real name was Kerry McKee.

'Trace,' came the acknowledgement, above the noise of the sliding lock.

Lorraine and Tracy were over by the pegs completing the manoeuvre of reinserting a stud into an infected earlobe. 'Gordon Bennett, it's agony!'

'And *your* Mum made you have it done proper,' Lorraine teased. 'Bag of frozen peas and a safety pin, me, and no probs.' She pressed the last millimetre. 'Magic, our Maurice.'

'Fuckin' Ace, mush,' growled Tracy, coming out of her wince and impersonating a well-known boy in the year above us.

'Saw you and Windebank in there,' Lorraine winked at me. 'Ain't you got off with 'im yet?'

'No way,' I said, hoping the opposite would be true. I had stationed myself at the washbasins to check my eyeshadow in the mirror. I'd no idea what half an hour's dancing in that steamy atmosphere would have done to it, this being the first time I'd worn

121

the stuff for a real occasion rather than endless trial-runs in other girls' bedrooms. I needed to be sure before the slow dances started.

I looked in the mirror. Even in the unflattering orange-pink light reflecting from the tiles of the showers behind me, I looked nice: cheeks flushed, eyes bright, hair feathery. I'd had it layered that week, with a fringe, a new style for me. What's more, our neighbour's daughter-in-law, Pauline, had done it, not my Mum. I risked a smile, with teeth. Were the front ones perhaps showing signs of retreat? I was assiduous about my brace, my devotion to duty in this respect having a slightly hysterical quality, as if leaving it out for even a short while might instantly cause my teeth to ping out at once at still more bunny-ish angles. I'd had a considerable tussle with myself over the moral implications of not wearing it for the disco, surely short-termism and weakness of character of the first order. It must be better to suffer now, for the sake of my postponed but all the more deserved reward, my inevitable and un-vanquishable attractiveness.

I wasn't sorry at that moment, though. The implied liaison with Shaun Windebank and the noting of it by a star player like Lorraine Madgewick were both confirmation of my sense of well-being and impending arrival, even though the conversation swiftly moved on.

'Is Gail still in there?'

'Too busy snoggin Steve Penney, I reckon,' boomed Mucky from her cubicle.

'The little scrubber,' they clucked approvingly. Trace finished adjusting the well-filled bra under her checked cowboy shirt and they went out, shuffling their feet and jiggling their hips in readiness for the dance. When I'd hinted to Mum that my chest might be expanding a bit – admittedly rather wishful thinking on my part – and that I might be in need of... well... a bra, she'd offered to make me a pinafore dress to make them show less. No, Mum, not quite.

'Thought it was Fisher you wanted to go out with,' Mucky was trying to reverse the panda-effect where her mascara seeped incongruously into the freckles round her eyes. I denied it swiftly. I wasn't going to be caught out in hubris of that magnitude. Kevin Fisher was even higher up the scale of female social aspiration than Shaun Windebank. I knew what I was, however elated I might feel. There was a strict hierarchy to these things. In my own class, despite the sticking-out teeth, and latterly the brace, the still-flat chest and the nearer-to-light-brown-than-blonde hair, I nonetheless held the position of second best girl. This meant I could be the romantic object of several boys in my class and the subject of gossip and speculation with regard to these, could receive emissaries and enter into negotiations as to whether I would agree to go out with one or another of them – this state being purely theoretical since in my case there was no prospect of going anywhere or even meeting up out of school, distance not permitting. It simply meant having proprietorial feelings of attachment and intimate chats when we should have been working, and the potential for hand-holding and even kissing at school-organised events, until such time as one of us chucked the other.

The first best girl was Sharon Cordner, a friend of mine and not at all conceited in her election. Having white-blonde hair, two renowned older sisters in the school and a father who owned a motorbike shop, she had indeed had little choice about it. She had the pick of boys in our class, and in fact had been going out appropriately with the first best boy for over a year. However, while I was definitely a league player rather than an international, Sharon's position meant that, should she choose, she could select her next partner from among that constellation, of which an association with Shaun Windebank brought me to the brink.

It was only the brink, mind. He was a bit of an acquired taste, Shaun, but I liked him. He was slightly chubby and tended to clown about, but I thought he had energy and genuine wit. He was one of those who instigated catch-phrases of his own, and made up words for things and situations. The reason everyone knew him was because he was funny, and self-advertising, and because his big brother was hard, and reportedly carried a knife.

'Are you going to let Windbag kiss you?' Mucky pursued. It occurred to me for the first time that Mucky, who made a threesome with Sharon and me, who was such a fixer of liaisons between others and in so many people's confidence, received no offers on her own behalf. She was scrawny and feisty rather than voluptuous, certainly, but she was so knowledgeable and lively, possessed so much of what, in magazines, was called *personality*, as well as a lot of fashionable clothes, that I'd never noticed.

'Well, *are* you?'

'I might do.'

'What, *French* kissing?'

I tried to cover my ignorance, leaning forward and squinting at my left eyebrow in the mirror, trying to think of some reply other than 'I might do' again.

'You know, with his tongue inside, wiggling it about. *Yuk, I* wouldn't do it!'

'Ugh,' I agreed. 'Messy job!' but I knew at once that the big-league girls *did* do it, knitting tongues in endless snogs in the corners of rooms. I had a sudden image of standing in the darkened front-room at Grampy's beneath the lampshade and its unlit bulb as he tipped back my head.

Wouldn't she be surprised if she knew? I thought, feeling odd and gleeful at the same time. Wouldn't they *all* be surprised – that I'd been doing it for *ages*. I knew more about it than *any* of them!

* * *

By the time I got to Grampy's it was past nine.

'Where *wus* you?' he shouted. 'I been worried sick. Yer mum said just after eight, that's what she said.'

I didn't tell him about stopping for chips with the others on Highlands Road.

'The disco was late finishing,' I told him. 'Some of us had to help put the chairs back in the Hall.'

'It's *late*. There's all kinds o' fellas out there, muggers an' whatnot. You oughta be *careful*. There's *all* sorts.'

He raised the curtain on the deserted street, the orange street-lamp light drizzling down on the bungalows and their hydrandgea-ed gardens.

'It says in the paper, old fella got 'it over the 'ead. It's not safe for young girls to be stoppin' out.'

'Sorry,' I said. 'Is there anything to eat?'

'Don't you sorry me,' he said, grabbing hold of me under the armpits, hoisting me off the floor and kissing me hard but off-centre.

'There's a doughnut,' he said. 'Come in the kitchen.'

I dashed ahead of him, rooting in the bread bin. I had the doughnut out of its paper bag and stuffed in my mouth by the time he had laboured down the hall after me.

'*Gurr,* you got me puffed,' he wheezed.

I bolted the doughnut, nipped round behind him and down the hall to the bathroom before he'd caught his breath. I had to clean my teeth after so much sugar, I told myself virtuously, leaning over the sink, eyes level with Grampy's spare set of teeth dangling in a glass of water on the windowsill. Damn it, I'd have to come out of the bathroom to get my bag with my brace in.

I opened the door a crack, but Grampy seemed to have gone back into the sitting room. I slunk out, grabbed the bag, and darted back in, pulling the door on my foot. I *had* to wear my brace. Some unwritten future in which my teeth would not stick out depended on it.

Seconds away, round two. Standing by the fire, pulled against his chest, he kissed me again, though I refused to open my mouth. I was having the same odd feeling I'd had at that moment of realisation in the changing rooms, but with the logic in reverse. Snogging wasn't something people did with their Grandads. *That* wasn't something I could imagine *anyone* I knew doing.

'Come an' keep yer ol' Gramp warm,' he said, holding me away for a moment. I wriggled my arms but he didn't loosen his grip. 'Gi' us a kiss and lend us a bob.'

'I can't, I've got my brace in.' I pulled away, successfully this time.

'Keep yer ol' Gramp warm,' he repeated, jerking his head towards the hallway and trying to take my hand. Did he mean *his* room? In *his* bed? He'd never suggested anything like that before.

'Goo'night then,' I said, half out the door, pretending not to understand, not sure I had, not understanding even what it meant if I had.

'It can't make a baby. I'm too old.'

'I've got my brace in,' I insisted, already gone.

I went into the spare room, where I'd slept before, though never without my brother and sister. I heard nothing to suggest that he was following. His wheeze always gave him away, regular like an unoiled see-saw. I pushed the door to the point where it always stuck, then gave it an extra shove so that it shut completely. I held the handle and shoved again to make sure it had clicked.

I went to bed with my clothes on, even my shoes, but I felt untroubled as I fell asleep. In the bottom drawer of my chest of drawers at home, underneath the spare blankets for the bed, I'd hidden Grampy's Christmas present. I usually got him mint humbugs and thermal socks, but this year I'd seen something special in the new section in Blunden's in the village. It was called Delicatessen, in red writing over the cheese counter and the fancy fridge. Chrystallised ginger, whatever that was, in a slim brown box decorated with splayed fans, bright, delicate and oriental-looking in pink, blue and orange. For some reason Mrs Blunden had nestled the box in straw. The combination of old-fashioned, old man sweetie-ness with the Chinese theme made it perfect for Grampy, and the waves of satisfaction, lying there thinking about it, sent me off to sleep, snatches of *Rocket Man* replaying in my head.

Starred Man

NO USE NOW, ME. I'M BUGGERED. WENT OVER this morning. No time
to dress. She's only overt road ye see. I used to see er when she were
expectin bairn like, up that road every day wit green frock sailin
out, an arms goin. Every day steamin upt road wi a great belly out
front. I like that. Shows she took care on erself. Kept erself fit. Used
to see er, as I say, but we never come to speakin till aftert bairn were
born. Bairn as some funny name – Zashka, Zoshka. From a book
most like. I like that. Folk should tek note what they reads on. No
it weren't from a book. She told me. She were workin there aforet
bairn came, Russia, or Poland. I like that, folk travellin a bit, seein
things clear for theirselves, learnin languages.

Our Gillian studied languages. She could speak three languages
afore she were married. Worked in Germany afor't bairns came. Er
usband, e's top man at Ewlitt Packard, in is division like. D'ye know
it? Big firm. Ead office is in Germany like, but they as a big plant over
at Earswick. E's top man there now is Erich. The've three bairns. All
swimmers. Eldest's already started on languages at school.

I can speak Russian miself like, knew quite a lot at one time,
though I've forgot it a now. Aden dvah tree, that's countin. I told er.
I counted for er in Russian. Learnt it off Russkies int war. We used
to stop wi em up on Bear Island, fittint ships, for Murmansk. Grand
lads wer't Russkies. Better'nt Yanks to us, friends like. Yanks was
right nice lads – but allus seemed to our way o thinkin as they was
showin off, bletherin about money, ex*aggerat*in.

Right keen on money we Yanks, leastway ones I worked wi. I
were weldin, mekkin cars, in Chicago afor't war. First war mind
now. Second were summat else. Whent war come the said it were

127

nowt, over bi Christmas an a that. Ant Yanks didn't care, Germans or British. You're a right, Bill, the said, starred occupation. You stop on ere, mek some dough. You'll drive one o these out o ere come a year.

I didn't want no bloody *Cadillac*. Come back on a liner to Southampton to enlist. I'd not o bin conscripted like on account o me bein starred man. I'd to work mi passage mind, no money fort fare. Three on us the was.

Well it were ammerin away int engine room mornin noon an night, an it were damned ot. Ye'd to put rags roun ye – ere and ere – an the come off wringin. Well appen some important fella – brigadier or summat – ears on us chaps workin our way ome to enlist like, an e as us called upstairs an e says we're fine lads an a that. We s'll hef to get you out o that engine room, e says. We s'll need all our strength fort Front, e says.

I'm not avin that, I says, an neither would tother chaps. We'd not sit still in a' that water, we'd to work it *some*'ow.

Mind it were offa, that ding an clatter – we were right glad to get to Southampton. I were lucky, though, when I enlisted. The needed a fitter an welder right away, in Scotland first off, fort convoys, then Murmansk.

Well int finish the left it to Merchant Navy lads an I went to France. But the's no sense speakin on it. Mud an such. Meks everythint same. Ye gets *con*fused. If ye've ad it ye'll know wi' out my sayin – don't matter where you was or what it were. Everythin what's that bad ist same.

I told er that. She comes over wit bairn an I mek er coffee. Or I tek over one o mi custards an she brings backt dish a washed up. Bairn's a little redhead. Mind, Edna says it's *fashionable* now. She's in most days is Edna. The're *too* good. Mi family's *too* good.

But I wanted to tell ye oft swimmin races we ad, int harbour like, when I were convalescin. Bloody great concrete mole goin out intot sea, an the set up marker buoys an whatnot for them races. I were allus a swimmer, since a lad. We used go up Tang All Beck them days. It were right water for swimmin. The've kept a bit of it int Park now. She goes there wit bairn. Edna says it's nobbut a trickle nowdays, an dirty, pram wheels an that. I can't get there now. Course there were none o them ouses. Milton Street wer't end o York them days, nobbut fields while Osbaldwick. I'd to exercise dogs in them fields afor't war.

But what was I tellin ye? I'm all over... oh yes, well, ole arbour were rigged out for them races, an it were grand to be int water after a that mud. So I won tfirst race. Ant second. We were just goin fort relay, Jack Ainsley – e were a grand swimmer, bit short ont forward stroke, but a ead on im, like a bullet, a great finisher – e were fort first leg. An I were a ready whent ead man, Colonel like, e steps up.

'Come on, Beard,' e says. 'Let's see you.' So I swims mi part like. But that's not enough, an e as me do a kinds o stuff, out to tplatform, an tother side ot mole, in an out them damned buoys. An I'm thinkin, what about tbloody race?

Seems these senior officers what were stationed there all time ave it in mind to old these kind o races regular, knock up a proper team o sportsmen, race em against a comers. An the wants me an a couple others – Jack Ainsley, there wer't pick o good swimmers there that day – to old us back like, for swimmin races.

I says no chance. I coudn't ave a cushy job like that, y'see. Ead officer e calls me a damn fool. Sergeant says, when e eard, that's right patriotic of ye, Bill, sneerin like, but I says I weren't a fool *that* way. I went back, till int finish I ad malaria four months. A lot o lads ad it. Medicine's worst part on it, an I got confused. Walked over a lot o dead bi that time.

I'm not keepin ye, am I – stood bletherin a day at street gate? Can't seem to get no further, y'see, since I ad that trouble we mi insides last year. Ye"ll ave to excuse me – I'm buggered I am. Folk are that good, mind. Which street was it ye said ye were lookin for? I'm not keepin ye am I? *She* allus stops. Seems right interested like, asks me what I done an that. I told er – it's true like – mi last job were two year ago, I ad it a year, warden fort city walls. I'd to walk round twalls last thing, mekkin sure no one were up there an a were well, an lock up when I come to each Bar. Bootham first, ant Micklegate last.

Well, the thought I were sixty-five when I took it, but when the found as I were ninety-three the said the couldn't kip me. I said why not, I'd done it a year, but the said as ow it'd not be allowed. First cushy job I ever ad an the gi me mi cards.

We ad a good laugh at that we did. She laughs lovely. Keeps erself well I reckon. Well afore that I were lifeguard an instructor at Baths for twenty year after I retired. The were new then at Barbican. Loads o young uns used to come. Mind, it were beautifully made that pool, a good big un. I never saw such clear water – ant tiles picked out ont bottom – not too much o that – what is it, I've gone an forgot word again? – *chlor*ine, that's it, so ye can *see*t water while ye're swimmin. I tell em, ye as to keep a clear ead when ye're swimmin. Ye've all that water comin at ye – threshin an foamin – in yer eyes an ears. A man as to tek a that water *through* im, an keep a clear ead. Then ye'll do a right.

No, I've not done bad misen – I were a fitter forty year. Rose to be top man ont floor at Braithwaites. But I wouldn't go no igher. Top man, Mr. Pritchard e were, e says to me as I could be promoted like, but I'd not go that way. The was good lads I worked wi an a, friends like. Elped out whent wife died. Ye're that *con*fused, like, int beginnin.

Was it long ago ye say? Nineteen fifty-two. December nineteen fifty-two. That's nigh on forty year, Mr. Beard, she says when I told er. I suppose it is that. I showed er a photograph o Kitty, though the're nowt alike int face. Er usband studies – we bin introduced. Bairn teks after er mother. The'll get on. I said that to Edna when she were over int week. Mi family's *too* good, the *are*. Tom an Edna are over most days, though I don't need em. I tell Edna to go to our Gillian an not be botherin about me. Our Gillian could do wi some elp wit bairns now she's wantin to get back to work. Started some o that *trans*latin for Ewlitt Packard. Usband's top man there now, did I tell ye? German firm, over at Earswick. Edna should be over *there* wi er own grandbairns, not worryin about me. I'm buggered I am, since I ad that trouble. Can't ardly move compared to what I used. Just stand at street gate.

Rose is over too – er what's a widda – er usband were invalid, fromt second war. The've two bairns, both done well. Susan's a nurse at big city ospital in Leeds, an Colin, e's summat wi computers – what's it the call im? – troubleshooter, that's it. E's ead of is team, goes round sortin other folk's problems wit computer. Whenever owt goes amiss, it's im as knows what to do. I'd a card one time, from a mate o mine in Ull. Thought it were right nice. Wrote ont address: 'Bill Beard and family, Best o't First Division.'

Went over this mornin, didn't ave time to dress. Must a bin early, for the weren't up. I've come about job I said. Oh, Mr. Beard, come in, sit down. I saw it int paper I said, but cord from mi dressing gown were a caught int fender and she'd to elp mi wi that. The advertisement, int paper. What kind of job was it for, she asked me? Qualified fitter, with experience, reliable. I'm yer man, I said. Er usband come in, shook ands, I said about job, what I've done like. She's int kitchen mekkin cups o tea, she's phoned to our Edna. Er usband's askin me summat – I'm sorry I never can remember is name. You'll ave to excuse me. I'm buggered I am. David, is it? Ah, *David...*

Field Study

I SEE THEM AS THEY COME OUT OF the trees into the cornfield, ducking under the wire. There's a stile, but they come out further up. The way from the bus-stop goes along the edge of the copse. I'll catch the same bus, only lower down the hill, when I go to college next year.

The boy has a stick, striking the bushes with it, and the nettles too I suppose. The boy comes first, swishing his stick, taking big strides. She follows after. I've a feeling he's not letting her catch up.

She has on a wine-red dress, the kind you get from the Indian stall in Gosford Market, the kind my Mum won't let me buy, says I'd look like a blooming hippy, a flower-power child. Well, that's the *idea* isn't it? The dress is a lovely colour, makes warm hollows as she walks or bends to the wire. She has a proper bust – not like me – so the material falls all floaty in pleats and shadows. She's got cowboy boots too, and a straw bag with books sticking out. She looks a bit like one of those French postcards, sort of old-fashioned with her hair up and wispy bits by her ears. You know, the ones with girls all rosy, with old-fashioned lace and doves – *and* cornfields come to think of it – and big straw hats. They take them with a special lens. Any case, the colours she's wearing are too strong – you need pastels for that kind of card – but you know what I mean. She still can't reach him, though she's put out her hand and saying something. I don't know what *he's* got on. Jeans, I think, and a black leather jacket.

The corn has still a kind of green haze about it – not *in* it exactly, but hovering – like it does just before it turns. I like to come up here, have done ever since we moved this side of the village last year. Before that we lived on the Estate, nearer the middle. I was up the

133

Rec all the time with my friends. Now it's more reading. I did miss it a bit in the beginning, but Dad says, what's the use being a builder if you don't build for your own? Dad likes to make the most of what's given him.

What's the use having fourteen brothers if you don't put your muscles together? That's another one of his. They have this building firm, see. Tanfield Bros. Not all of them, just seven. Not Uncle Lenny. None of them would want *him* where money's concerned. Dad's the eldest, so he's sort of the boss. *Fourteen* brothers. Two of my uncles are younger than me. I've only got three, fortunately – brothers that is – and a sister. None of them'll go to college, I don't reckon. I'm the only one that's interested. We have a lot of these what's the use-type arguments nowadays, because his point of view is very different from mine. I mean, he's glad I'll be going to college and that – if I get my predicted grades – that's using what you got. Just so long as I don't start dressing like some grubby student, he says. But he doesn't see why I have to take it so far, why I don't go out like Trish and Darren do. I tell him I *like* reading.

'What, them *telephone* books?'

He always calls them that, says they're that thick.

'It's only Tess,' I say. It still gives me a thrill calling it 'Tess' like that, like we're on first name terms. But he goes and says 'Tess who?', and makes me feel stupid. Tess of the *D'Urbervilles*, of course – but I know I can't say it in such a way as to make *him* feel small. It'll sound daft even to me with him hearing. 'Tess of the *what*? Any relation to Hound of the Baskervilles?' That's what he'll say. So I pretend I haven't heard him and sweep out. Hound of the Baskervilles has been on the telly – he hasn't *read* it of course. Actually, come to think of it, neither have I. Dad boasts the paper's all the reading matter he's needed in years.

'Ain't that right, Flo?'

He often calls my Mum 'Flo', from the Andy Capp cartoon. He used to call me it too sometimes, when I was younger and used to help him. Only help he gets now is with the crossword.

'What's the use having a clever daughter if she don't give you a hand with the crossword in the paper?'

So I have to do it. I don't like crosswords, any case. When I got a clue wrong the other day he was on about it for *hours*.

'Let her be, Ray,' my Mum says.

But even then he's on at me to go up the village and help one of my Aunties. My Mum's one of twelve and all, so there's no shortage of *them*. Honest, we're related to half the village.

Round Christmas and Auntie Yvonne and Uncle Derek's twenty-fifth, we had a family get-together in the Victory Hall. I brought my friend Suzanne from Gosford. I know her from school.

'Are those *all* your family?'

She couldn't believe it, except we all look so alike. Apart from Angie, a little girl my Auntie Margaret adopted when her mum and dad were killed in a car smash. Suzanne said that every time anyone was explaining to her who was who, they'd say 'oh and that's Angie – she's *adopted*.' As if they needed to, Suze said, the kid was the only blond one in the whole room. She thought it was ever so funny. We're all dark, skin and hair, and quite a lot of us are curly. Dad jokes as how we were Gyppos not far back. It explains Uncle Lenny, he says. Sometimes I wish I could go right away.

This is as far as I get. My track follows the bottom edge of the cornfield. Down left there's a beautiful view, stomping behind the pylons along the valley. Panoramic I think you call it. But I mostly look the other way. I prefer views *upwards*, with things appearing over the tops of other things, clumps of trees, barns and hedgerows sliding into sight above the corn, and the woods a lopsided collar against the hill.

They can't see me, and perhaps that's what I like. A clump of scraggy ash trees adrift in the corn hides me from them. They're not looking, any case.

She's got him to stop. I didn't think he would, but he's turned, leaning on a post at the edge of the field. Her arms are very white to the elbow, where the sleeves of the red dress come, and she's moving them a lot, reaching forward. He has one of those Zippo lighters, silver, and keeps flipping the lid open with his thumb and clicking it shut, but he doesn't light a cigarette. There's a tobacco tin in his shirt pocket, I can see, but he doesn't go near that. She's speaking very fast, though the words don't carry, bent forward with her arms going. Pleading with him, I reckon, or arguing something. Not having much effect as far as I can see, his whole body and his face are kind of leant back away from her, as if his own stick were leant against a wall. I can't really make out his face properly from here, but it's like he's sneering – he really doesn't think much of her.

Which is odd, because I've seen them come down that path before, so pressed together there were no gaps between them, their legs working like in a three-legged race, only faster than they meant to, going downhill. When I saw, my insides gave a great fierce jump right down to my knees, and I thought, I *want* that. I want that.

Her voice is going up and down. It must be great to have proper grown-up arguments like that, real passionate ones about real subjects, about love. Of course you have to have a real boyfriend first. I haven't yet, but when I *do* ... . There's Nicky of course – in fact I ought to be getting back in case he comes round. They've made a serial of *Sons and Lovers* – it's one of our set books – and he bikes over from Gosford to watch it at my house, then we discuss it. It's good of him to come all that way, nigh on ten miles I reckon. My family tease me and call him my boyfriend, but they don't understand anything. People think just because we go about together all the time we must be going out. It's so simplistic.

I mean, he *is* pretty keen on *me*. He declared himself, as they say in books, a few months back. Of course I already knew. It was ever so embarrassing, but I had to say I'd no feelings for him in that way, though I'd gladly remain friends. I think our friendship's really important, I said, and I truly value it. It ought to be possible for men and women to be close and understanding, without anything else. We have so much in common, and we talk about books so fruitfully and so well. It's an intellectual thing really, a disinterested affection. I'm sure it's very rare, I told him, and we must take care not to spoil it. He accepted that, though I know he'd still like more. It's nice to be wanted, and I felt really bad doing it – but when it's love you just *know. I* will, any case. From what I know about love, it doesn't creep up on you slowly. I don't mean it has to be at first sight or anything, but you just *know*.

Afterwards I lay on my bed all dreamy, gazing at my posters, not seeing them, just *having* the feeling that came from what had happened, and thinking *this* is a feeling to have. Naturally part of it was quite uncomfortable – I could see I'd really knocked him – but what else could I say? Yet part of me was full of a strange happiness. I could see the future all glittery and vague sort of floating in the room before me. There are so many feelings I haven't had yet.

Of course he's quite *sweet*. He'll do anything for me, and he has a sort of beady, *blackbirdy* look sometimes. He reads that late he's got these brown shadows under his eyes like little bruises. Ever so sweet – but just not boyfriend material somehow, there's no way round it. He's not tall enough, for a start. I mean I know I'm too old for all that girls' magazine rubbish, where boyfriends are to be met with at ice-rinks and funfairs, labelled *dishy* and kissed thinking *mmmmmm* in a bubble. I saw through all that a long time ago. I really should be getting back, though, just in case Nick calls. One day I'll meet a boy who really sees, sees all of me, and we'll fall in love and stay together always. Perhaps at college it'll happen. He'll be one I can really respect, who knows how to look through me right to the bottom and loves me completely.

He's pulled away from her, but she's stalled him again, hand on his arm, speaking urgently. He's got his stick between his two hands, butting it at her sideways like he's a lion-tamer with a folded whip. Now he's tugged himself free and he's away in an arc breaking out from the edge of the field. The corn tramples easily, so you can see the swathe where he's gone. She follows, keeps to the edge, then wades out. His head turns on his body above the corn. He says something to her, one more thing. And she stops.

You can see the knuckles of his two fingers above the black leather shoulder, looped through the bag hanging down his back, and he's off up the ridge through the corn. The same wind lifts the hair at the back of his neck as ripples the corn.

All of a sudden she goes down, all uneven like several different heavy objects into the corn. She's crying, I can hear her, over and over the same, and really loud.

'Come back, please come back.'

The air seems to be creaking with that sound, split by it in many places. It's like a lark's singing, as if it came from *above* the air and rained down in splinters through it. I can almost *see* the air grown buzzing and fuzzy, like when you look up for larks too high to find.

And I know she can smell that sour rusty smell of earth, low down among the stalks denting her knees. I'm sure she smells it like a colour she's mixed with her tears, and that she breathes it all, her wet face, her own words, the corn, the sky, from one place, crushed in the brittle stems, below.

I'm looking where he's gone, gulped into the swell of the land above the ridge, and the air heaving greyly over the corn. Doesn't she know he's gone? It's not for him. She must know he can't hear her. It's for herself, for the air, the prickling stalks of corn, because it's like those words are this moment's name.

In the space above where she is I keep seeing her break up again into disjointed squares oddly arranged on one another the moment before she falls. Like that Cubist painting *Woman Coming Downstairs*. I'm starting to take an interest in modern art, you see. I thought it was time. The girl hasn't got up yet. Still, if I had a bust like she's got, I don't think I could stay sad about *anything* for long.

Tea for the Rent Boy

IT WAS SO COLD WE HAD TO TAKE a cup of tea down to the rent boy in the square below my ex-husband's flat. My daughter said we should, and it seemed to me she was right. Helpful, not too patronising. Something he could accept without interrupting the flow of his custom any more than the roll-up he was smoking, perched on the low part of the wall at the edge of the car-park, half hidden by the glossy vehicles of the solicitors. The other kind of solicitors. The kind in heated offices with filing cabinets and sash windows. The kind who don't look so pale and paper thin it's as if the wind has blown through them and left a liquorice tinge to every part of exposed skin. The kind that have a single crease to their trousers, rather than the tightest of tight jeans that still appear too big, adhering to the legs like cling-film rewrapped around its tube.

'Trust you to pick the pink light district to buy your classy pad in, Dad.'

Rosa's thirteen and knows her onions when it comes to the seamy side of life, or likes to think she does. Certainly the nature of the young man's occupation would never have occurred to me. I'd just have thought he had to come outside to smoke at odd hours all day every day, and often at night.

Still, it was awful cold, so cold that it might not seem insulting, more like the only thing to do. I took the steaming mug down, with a couple of thin twists of sugar pilfered from the coffee shop at work, which I'd found in my bag, in case he took that, and gambled that he liked it with milk. A very British solution, ours, in any case:

'I'm twenty-one though I look about sixteen and I need to sit here in the freezing cold because I have to get fucked by at least five

139

businessmen in the next two hours if I'm to feed my heroin habit.'

'Have a cup of tea, dearie: everything looks better after a nice cup of tea.'

Instead, I stuck to 'here you go,' 'thought you might like this,' or 'you look chilly and it's nice and hot' – don't make him have to purchase his cuppa with small talk, for God's sake – and he stuck to 'cheers' with a grimace that worked better than a smile. Walk away quickly – no obligation on either side – and back indoors. He left the cup on the steps after, nodded up at the window to make sure we'd seen, so he obviously knew which one was ours. We didn't exchange introductions until about two months into our ritual. Ralph, such a rent boy name – how do I know that? – and, anyway, probably not his real name. How do I know that either? Like a stage name; he's probably called Calum or Craig or something. Ryan – he looks like a Ryan – or maybe a Kyle. Close up he had a smattering of pale purple acne and the tobacco stains on his fingers looked more like old ink-spots. Max-Pedar thought the whole tea thing ridiculous – but then he thought everything I did was ridiculous – wrong-headed or ill-intentioned, or unlikely to achieve the outcome I desired, even if that were acknowledged to be sound. Certainly not what he'd have done, which amounted to the same thing and went without saying. Except nowadays he was keeping up a barrage of charm in my direction and therefore didn't mention it – which meant he could have exercised such self-restraint before, had he seen the need.

* * *

That must be five months ago now, it's still just as cold, and I'm standing in the same position at the window, looking at the seagull in masterful profile on top of Lord Gordon's newly scrubbed statue, the granite frontages of the town houses on the far side of the square, the spire of the Catholic Cathedral. An Archibald Simpson square, don't you know? They know it in the two discreet estate agents' situated at opposite corners down below. There's no sign of buds on the trees, or of Ralph on the wall near the parked cars. The council van hasn't yet come round with the spring window boxes, part of their 'offer', for a small retainer, in this 'centrally located, newly residential district'. The evergreens in the winter box look a bit bedraggled, but mostly OK.

Behind me, Max-Pedar has his laptop on the breakfast bar, surrounded by stills, which he's spread out so he can see them all at once, engrossed in the slide show images on the screen, turning periodically to shuffle through the printed images for comparison. I haven't finished the mug of coffee he made me, but see this is a chance to try and get through to Sol, pick up my mobile from the glass coffee table. Straight to voicemail. Previously, I always assumed that if I didn't hear from him it was because he was having a good time. He'd call if he needed to. He's only in Glasgow, after all. Since he switched courses at the start of second year, though, after a lot of misery and soul-searching which he didn't share with me, at least not till afterwards, my sense of my robust boy off in the world, doing just fine without me, took a knock. Film Studies seems to suit him much better than Biology, but I find myself dwelling on how thin he is – always has been, but is he eating properly? Does he have enough friends? This new fragility I see in him, this belated vulnerability, is it a delayed reaction to the fiasco of my attempt to bring his father back into his life? Even though he didn't know half of what went on. I tried to keep that from him, at least. Still, children can punish themselves unconsciously for that kind of stuff. How old was he back then – only fifteen?

Max-Pedar looks up, briefly. 'You calling Sol? Give him my love.' He shuffles the photographs into a pile. 'I'll start cooking in a minute – just need to finish one thing... Where's Rosa?'

Rosa is in the shower – knowing that if she times it right she can avoid doing any clarinet practice before the food is served. I look around the flat, the granite-topped breakfast bar, the long-legged, Italian, steel-framed chairs, the Miro print over the mantelpiece, the black marble living-flame fire, the freshly painted white cornices edging the high ceiling, the modern take on a chandelier. This being a listed building, the developers got in genuine craftsmen and interior designers, consulted the new owners every step of the way. Max got to pick everything. I'm glad it's nice, I think. I'm glad he has this. For a while it made me angry. So angry I avoided him altogether. Wherever did that rage go?

Max-Pedar is tidying away the photographs, but keeps stopping to consider individual shots. He's wearing the dark jumper Rosa persuaded him to buy last week. It has a kind of low polo-neck, and I can't decide whether this makes him look like a dentist or a French cat-burglar.

He looks up. 'Tell Rosa she needs to get out of the bathroom and do some clarinet practice. She's been in there a good hour.'

I don't move. 'You tell her.'

Your flat, your call, I think. I don't want to do all the parental policing tasks. She's on my watch all week, after all. He gets enough credit for the superior bathroom facilities and the wide screen TV. These must be the pictures for the book to get this kind of attention. The image he's holding is a long-ago shot, a close-up of pale orange cloudberries shivering against springy russet lichen and yellow grasses, taken on the dry bog above the farm on Kvaløya. Streamers of white cloud flare into the sky from the line of the horizon, but the foreground creates an almost abstract, patterned design. Max-Pedar has always been very rigorous about observing boundaries between his commercial and what he calls his own work. I have only myself to blame that I never did the same.

We first came to this city when Max got a six-month contract for the Marine Lab's big Arctic exhibition. He'd had to take leave from his employers down in England to do it, but it had enabled him to go freelance, with follow-up publicity for oil companies, documenting sustainable development projects. As soon as it became clear that Motorskills was going to be a success, bringing in some modelling portraiture and film agency work as well – airbrush artistry, Max called it – we relocated properly, renting a ramshackle house near the park. It was cheap, the children had lots of friends nearby and there were deer in the garden spring and autumn. One year there were two fawns born in the spinney between the compost heap and the row of old garages. Max-Pedar ascribed my continuing contentment with the status quo, my failure to get excited about owning a place of our own, to lack of drive.

'The trouble with you,' he'd say – he started a lot of sentences that way – 'is you've no future tense.' Depending on his mood, he'd put it down to personality or to my lower class background.

'At least I have a present tense,' I'd counter. 'You're only happy planning and projecting – always *furthering* something.' Well, he owned a place now all right.

Looking at the top of his head, bent over the laptop, his hair is very black still, just the tiniest streaks of grey at the temples. It isn't Sami hair really, whatever his father might have liked to say, too fine and wavy. Whenever Duncan had wanted to goad Max-Pedar's mother, he'd call her family a bunch of inbred reindeer herders. 'Shake her family tree, and you never know what will drop out,' he used to say, disappearing behind his newspaper as she exploded, as though her response was of no possible relevance. Anyone else might have meant it as a joke. Perhaps anyone but Inga-Bodil would have taken it as such. Perhaps she had, at first. Max-Pedar always said Norwegians don't do irony, that he'd learned his at boarding school.

His hair is growing out a bit, I notice, but he's never changed his haircut, not even now, when everything about him, from his flat to his clothing is smart and new. Not since the days at prep school, when the once-a-term visit to either of the two local barbers, whether Lance the Lawnmower or Hacker Hodges, invariably produced an identical result. When we were first together he started to let it grow a little longer and allowed the curls to develop at the back and round his ears, but it was basically still the same style. Perhaps this was part of the hippy influence, the detour in his life he attributes to me.

These are the things you know about someone with whom you've shared a life, not just your past together, your children's childhoods, but each other's childhoods, your family histories, your parents' youthful meetings, their marriages, happy or otherwise, their wartime stories, distinctive places and collective lives among the people they come from. It's too much. It's all in the room, in this spanking new room, simultaneously, right now, floating there above the parquet like layers of mist rising in the morning across the moorland bogs of Kvaløya. At any moment, without even moving, I can wander into one of these furls of white vapour. Even standing still, a strand might wreathe and creep and envelop me at any time. I feel overwhelmed at the thought, and pick my way over to the kettle to make myself another coffee.

'Want one?' I ask Max, but he's concentrating too hard to reply.

I usually describe Max as my ex-husband, for simplicity. We got together when Sol was only a toddler, but we never did the whole marriage thing, to the horror of his parents.

'Why would you not give to your kids two passports?' Inga-Bodil had cried, uncomprehending.

Perhaps that was it. Rosa could have had a Norwegian passport, but Sol couldn't. Even so, we'd had those two beautiful hot summers, while Mormor and Morfar were still alive, the orcas crossing the fjord while Sol was fishing from the kayak, camping on Sommarøy, the crackle of the Northern lights over the tent, Rosa walking Birk and Larka, Mormor's huskies, along the shore, using all her strength to haul them away from the terrified lemmings they'd flushed out from under the flat, grey stones.

I don't know which of us got the most satisfaction from seeing the children relive the benefits of our two childhoods, pooling our familial resources, even though Max had always said he wasn't very Norwegian at all, insisting boarding school had knocked that out of him. When I was a child, we went every summer to a borrowed caravan in the Dales. Max-Pedar thought the Dales were sweet. Scotland, now, that was a place Max-Pedar respected, felt he had a right to, because of his father, though he'd grown up in the Midlands himself. Raised on his mother's tales of the Shetland Bus and Wartime resistance derring-do, as a child, he said, he thought of Scotland as a country of gritty heroes. When we got here, he discovered the Mac in his surname counted for little, and only his unusual Christian name saved him from the damaging assumption that he was English. Max was enraged but never referred to his Scottish background again.

Like a lot of things though, I think to myself, my employment for example, though not to be confused with Max's 'own work' category, things turn out to be pleasant in a different way than expected. Even in the beginning it never felt like an office job to me. I liked the art students, the friendly, funny women I worked with, the lecturers – except the photography professor who fancied himself something rotten and we all knew to be a dick, but who was wary around me because he knew Max-Pedar's work. Max did a couple of guest lectures there a few years back. I didn't like that. I thought it was my space: the kilns on the third floor, the slight smell of turpentine in the corridors wafting into the big, open-plan office, the view from the window, not directly in front, but just to the right of my desk, so I could look out at the full-leaved trees hanging heavy over the bend in the river as if peering at a landscape round the edge of an easel.

I'm not a naturally organised person, whatever that may be, and my clerical skills at the start were patchy, but I soon side-stepped into student advising, international exchange admissions and, latterly, events organisation, the much-vaunted public engagement initiative. It was an aptitude I didn't know I had, though not so different from being a mother really – imagining all the things that need to be done, writing lots of lists and then doing them, delegating when necessary and keeping other people on board by talking to them a lot so they know what's happening. Simple.

With any luck I'll be able to get my hours up to the level of a seventy-five percent contract next year and be almost solvent. The whole common-law thing means I'm entitled to precisely zilch that Max doesn't care to give me, even though at the time of the split we said we wanted to do it all amicably. Still, I'm the one that called time on our relationship, so he gets to be the hard-done-by party, swish, city-centre pulling pad and all, while I get the penury and the drudgery, taking on more and more hours to cover the rent, ferrying Rosa back and forth, since Max doesn't drive – the only good part being that I don't have to live with him, have him breathing down my neck. Which raises the question, leaving aside the old playing happy families thing for Rosa, why am I here so damned often myself?

* * *

Rosa moseys into the room in a bath-robe and towel turban, mobile phone clamped to her ear. 'So I said to her "borrow your *own* wellies!"' She slumps into the cushions on the sofa, curls her feet under her. 'I *know* – the sticky stuff on those cards – why? *Why?*'

There's a short pause while the person on the other end says some more.

'Well, she should have stuck to *aff*orementioned plan, then she'd be coming from home and wouldn't be needing my wellies at all.'

Rosa has a tendency to place the stress in a word differently than other people, but winningly, in a way that half-convinces the listener she's right. Certainly her peculiarities of pronunciation and emphasis tend to linger, as though they're preferable or part of a strange parallel lexicon.

'Kir, anyone?' Max-Pedar turns from the chopping board, wipes his palms down the green-and-white stripes of his new Lakeland apron.

Max-Pedar has recently bowed to pressure, mainly from Rosa, over his drinking – though he still denies there was ever any connection between having had a drink or three and the

unpleasant arguments which mysteriously arose. I don't need to drink every day, he'd say. I just like to. Rosa challenged him to prove it by never drinking on his own – so now anyone who comes through the door is prevailed on to join him.

'Yes please,' I say. He reaches into the fridge for the wine, placing the bottle on the counter with a flourish and fishes in the cupboard for the glasses. The cassis is on the rotating optic device that Max-Pedar and Rosa call The Magic Roundabout.

'Last week Dad tried to get Beccafinlayson and Eilidhnixon to join him in an aperitif,' Rosa enjoys grassing him up to me in his hearing. 'That's shocking, Dad – you know fine well they're under-age.' Rosa's friends think The Magic Roundabout way cool, a fact which she is not above relishing.

'As I recall,' says Max-Pedar, 'those two, along with the rest of your friends – Ross, is it, and Chris? – were quite happy to help themselves to the contents of The Magic Roundabout when I wasn't here – and made a serious dent in the vodka. Did you stop them? I don't think so. I've had to hide it when I go out, ever since.'

'It wasn't Chris, it was Danielrobertson, actually, and Danielcruickshank, oh, and Markbinnie.' When relating their exploits, Rosa always gives the names of her associates in full, enunciated like a single moniker.

'It wasn't even Aperitif Hour,' recalls Max-Pedar reproachfully. 'Little savages.'

Aperitif Hour is 6 o'clock, or, these days, with Inga-Bodil, anytime after midday, or even before that if someone has arrived by train or car from any distance away. Duncan would never have stood for that when he was alive. He always did his pre-six o'clock drinking in private. I was never quite sure whether the clink of ice in the glasses at that precise time of the evening was particular to his family or was yet another facet of class. In the beginning those kinds of differences between us were part of the fascination and the fun – like my thinking a D-J was a disc-jockey not a dinner jacket, or, horror of horrors, that gin went with orange squash rather than tonic – before it all became ammunition for the endless trading of caricatures between us.

My Mum has a sherry or two at Christmas and my Dad a swift half on a Friday after work with his mates, all blokes he was at school with. The Combined Trades, they call themselves, a Brickie, a Chippie, a Sparky and Dad. "Pete the Plunge," Les dubbed him, with the tag-line, "What he don't know about U-bends i'n't worth knowin'." Les isn't a brickie anymore, really. He's moved into roofing. Mum used to take us to the public library on a Friday night after her work, and we'd select our books and spend a bit of time reading at the big round table with the newspapers on it, under the eye of Auntie Maureen, the librarian, while Mum chose her titles and checked them out. Then we'd pile in the van and pick up our fish suppers on the way home. When we got in, the TV would already be on, warmed up, playing the signature tune for *Starsky and Hutch* or *Holmes and Yoyo*, whatever was the latest vaguely comic American cop-show, and Dad would be waiting, with the ketchup bottle upside down on the table and a big brown pot of tea.

Max-Pedar knows all this about me, all the childhood stuff, just as I do about him. I take my kir over to the window and sip it, a bit dizzy. There's a sharp crack, a vehicle backfiring on the other side of the square, and, just like that, I'm straight back there: the old blue van, Dad's van, we always called it, even though Mum drove it sometimes, with our surname on it in yellow writing, and the phone number, Malthwaite 457 339. In those days you didn't use the area code, I remember. Trying to get it to start on cold mornings: 'Let the choke out a bit more, love,' Dad would tell Mum; or the door handle that was a plastic cord inside the door – 'Give it a good old

147

jerk, love,' he'd say to me. Being next to the door was my job. Paul wasn't trusted to do this in case he leaned on the cord and fell out. I still hear his whine of complaint, bobbing with indignation at the unfairness. I can see it now, the elevated view through the slightly grubby windscreen, the dangling monkey behind the mirror, the yellow foam peeking through the tear in the black faux-leather that was always about to be patched but never was, and the debris of old sweet wrappers and carbon-copy receipts under our feet.

We didn't have a car, just the van, but Mum could walk to work at the old people's home. The Rest on Your Laurels Home, Uncle Les called it, with the monkey puzzle tree in the front garden in the street opposite the Rec. Once we were a bit older we would go up the Rec after school and wait for her shift to finish. When she stood in the back kitchen, we could wave to her from the top of the slide, and she'd nip across the road with two mugs of milk and a slice of sponge each, from the residents' tea. The swings were the ones on which I would later push baby Sol, liking the continuity even then.

Sol really likes the Combined Trades, especially Les, says he's a mine of information. When he was little, he treated them as a kind of four-in-one granddad, and he'll still go for a drink at the Three Tuns with them if we're ever down home, as they and he still call it, on a Friday night. An odd sight, gangly Sol with his pony tail, in his too-big, too-thin T-shirts heading down the road with four well-wrapped-up, elderly men, one grey-haired, one white and two in various stages of balding. I check my phone to see if I have a missed call, realise I've had it on silent by mistake the whole time.

The Combined Trades were unusual in that they managed to sustain themselves without working for the big power plant, simply serving the small town and the nearby villages.

'Yes, there's never been any doubt that your family's relentlessly local,' Max-Pedar said once. His gift for the memorable derogatory phrase reminded me of Duncan, though it was blasphemy to say so. Still, that's what a family is, this abundant storehouse of jumbled baggage. That's why Max-Pedar is Sol's dad in a way Ari never was.

'Where are my scrunchies?' Rosa holds the dark mass of curly hair on top of her head with one hand, groping in her ballet bag for hairgrips with the other.

Rosa never comments on whether I stay over, apparently noticing only so far as it assists or impedes her plans. She never seems to read anything into it. All kids want their parents to get back together, surely, but Rosa doesn't seem to. She has the best of both worlds.

'It's great to be in town, and for after school and that,' she'll say, 'but you, Sarah, really need to get a proper TV.'

It's a new thing with Rosa, using our first names when issuing instructions.

'I like our house – it's cosy, except when there's no food, and the lack of satellite channels,' is her assessment. 'You're quite handy for lifts,' she'll concede. It's also one of the perks of her new position to pass judgement on our respective parenting styles.

'You get a bit pissy, sometimes,' she tells me, 'but Dad's practically *Satan!*'

Not these days, I think now, watching him.

Rosa has reappeared in her preferred weekend wear, crop-top and t-shirt, with thick, black, dancers' tights under a skimpy skirt.

'Haven't you forgotten to put on a skirt with that belt you're wearing?'

'LOL, sooo funny, Dad. The old ones are the best, eh?'

Rosa puts her head on one side and pulls a sorrowful face at me.

'The other day I came to school with two plastic bags. The teachers think I'm like the suitcase kid, she says gleefully. They keep looking at me... Last week Mrs Innes hauled me up for wearing a non-standard school skirt, said it was more like a ballet skirt, a tutu. I've been wearing it since first year and they've only just noticed!' She is triumphant. 'This school's way too posh if I'm the most off-the-rails kid they've got.'

'Yeah, but you are kinda encouraging them, Rosa.'

'Everyone likes attention,' says Rosa smugly. 'I'm the sad child of a broken home, remember.'

'But you can't be the only one, surely, and your parents aren't at each other's throats. We come to Parents' Night and the school orchestra concert and everything. Together I mean.'

Rosa looks at me archly. 'Think how confusing that is – not just for them – for poor little old me. Clear signals are so important, Miss Teehan says.' She dances over to the mantelpiece. 'Got any bus money, Dad?'

Max-Pedar is squeezing garlic onto the steaming haricot beans. 'In the sheepie-bank, but it's lunchtime – don't go out now.'

Rosa has already emptied the china sheep of its coins. 'Calm your beans, I'm meeting Acey, and Beccafinlayson, but not till later.'

Max-Pedar's knife hovers over the ham, which he's taken from the oven and placed in its baking tray on the worktop next to the stove, filling the room with the scent of honey and cloves.

The doorbell rings. Max tuts.

'I'll get it,' I say.

It's Hazel from downstairs, wearing the velvetiest of suede thigh boots, hair scraped into a high, streaked blonde ponytail. 'Hello, pet – I said I'd drop this by.'

'Ooh, says Rosa over my shoulder, looking at two beige handles poking like bunny ears from the crepe in the open box. 'Is that the bag – *thank* you.'

Hazel regularly gives Rosa Louis Vuitton handbags and expensive body firming creams, probably thinking me a bit deficient in this department.

'There's an eye cream in there works a treat, Rosa pet – not that you've got my wrinkles to contend with. Gorgeous complexion, she has.' She turns to me, 'her Dad's colouring, bless her – your eyes.' Then, batting away the invitation: 'Can't stop – mess to sort out at work, and I'm needing a drive.'

Hazel is the owner-manager of the Private Eyes Club two streets away, and drives her Porsche along the coast road too fast for Rosa ever to be allowed to accept the regular offers of a ride. Rosa has dived into the crepe paper and is exclaiming over the bag.

'Tell her to pop over later,' she advises me, then to Rosa: 'You know I said I was having the boob job. Well, you should see the scars! That should put her right off,' she says confidentially to me, heading down the stairs, brandishing her tangerine fingernails in a twirly, over-the-head wave.

'All young people consider surgery,' says Rosa, knowingly, bearing her prize back to the sofa. 'Hazel's SOOO nice to me.'

'You sure it's a hand-me-down?

'Looks brand new to me.'

'You're scared of her, aren't you, Dad?'

'Course not!' Max laughs, forking more green beans onto Rosa's plate. 'Scared of powerful middle-aged Northern women in stilettos with fast cars, *moi*? What *are* you suggesting?'

'He so is,' says Rosa happily. 'Poor Maxy, your neighbours aren't quite as posh as you expected, are they? Apart from Theo.'

Theo is the teddy-bear shaped, Singaporean radiologist next door.

'Theo's very nice – and very tolerant of the racket you sometimes make. I don't have a problem with colourful neighbours. I'm a Bohemian, me.'

'Aye, right,' says Rosa.

'Go on, you know you love it,' I weigh in. 'All the meetings over – what are they called again? – shared factoring charges, storage space in the cellar, and ordering the window boxes. All part of the big home-ownership adventure!'

'I don't feel my efforts to be a good bourgeois householder are receiving the respect they deserve,' Max puts on an offended tone. He clears away the plates as Rosa finishes her beans. 'Now, would anyone like desert?'

'Afters,' says Rosa, glancing at me. 'Mum calls it afters, don't you, Sarah?'

'Sweet, desert, pudding – whatever,' Max doesn't rise to the bait and neither do I. Getting us to argue for her entertainment is part of Rosa's current skill set, though not one of those listed under that heading on her recent less-than-glowing school report.

'Seen Andy lately?' Rosa picks another topic for her purposes.

Andy bought the top flat as a buy-to-let, then moved in when his wife threw him out of the house in Bridge of Don for the fifth time.

'He has a girlfriend who stays over,' Rosa reports, ever the moralist, and as if I don't know who Andy is. 'Half his age, and a foot taller.'

'Don't be so judgemental,' Max-Pedar brandishes his latest gadget, which looks like a flame-thrower, at the crème brule. 'Who wants to see me do this?'

'Max likes Andy because he's an alky too,' Rosa observes, adding with relish, 'a pure drunkard.'

The week after Andy moved in, he showed up at Max's door at 3 a.m. clutching a bottle of whisky, and, having dozed off earlier in the day, apparently under the impression that it was three in the afternoon. At about 6 a.m. and two-thirds of the way through the Whyte and Mckays, Max was playing jazz CDs and Andy, claiming to be a virtuoso clarinettist, insisted on demonstrating using Rosa's instrument, which she'd left on the desk, out of its case.

'*You* let him.' There's still some mileage in this, even now.

'*You* left it out. Anyway, you like Andy.'

'I did – not anymore! You *know* why! I bet you never gave him my letter.' 'You're damn right I didn't. I did tell him you disapproved though.'

'What did he say?'

'He said he was really sorry, and sent you the chocolates, but the seagulls were driving him insane!'

'That's not an excuse. You should have shown him the letter. Where is it?'

'It's in the bedroom, on the bookshelf – but you can't go round actually sending things like that. It's hate mail.'

'Why not? He's a murderer! A *birderer*, in fact.'

'I have to get on with people... *Rosa!*'

She prances back into the room, flourishing the folded page – ANDY in capitals underlined three times, arrows pointing to the name bearing the inscription EVIL BIRD KILLER, PLAYBOY, FUGITIVE and DRUNK AS A SKUNK IN A FUNK – opening it out on the breakfast bar. Max clears away the plates and stacks them next to the dishwasher. On lined paper from her homework jotter:

TO ANDY!

I AM APALLED TO HEAR FROM MY FATHER THAT YOU WERE SHOOTING SEAGULLS [AND ALSO A PIGEON]! THAT IS CRUEL AND MEANS YOU HAVE NO HEART. YOU MAY THINK IT'S NOT SERIOUS BUT IT IS! IT IS A SIMILAR CRIME TO THE VIRGINIA SHOOTING! BIRDS HAVE FEEELINGS AND FAMILIES! YES, I BET YOU DIDN'T THINK OR CARE ABOUT THE [SCORED OUT] POOR FAMILIES OF THOSE SEAGULLS (OR THE PIGEON)! YOU ARE AN EVIL BIRD KILLER! I AM ONLY

13 AND IF I GROW UP TO BE A RADICAL EXTREME ANIMAL RIGHTS ACTIVIST THEN IT WILL BE YOUR FAULT. I HOPE YOU WILL NEVER, EVER DO THAT AGAIN. I'M DISAPPOINTED I THOUGHT YOU WERE NICE.

ROSA (DAUGHTER OF MAX, FLAT 8)

P.S.ALSO, I HEAR FROM HAZEL THAT YOU ONCE HIT A GUY OUTSIDE BELLA ITALIA. YOU ARE HORRIBLE. JUST HITTING SOMEONE FOR NO APPARENT REASON. THAT IS SHOCKING. YOU ARE A MEAN SEAGULL-SHOOTING, RANDOM-GUY HITTING, DRUNK MAN WHO TRIES TO PLAY OTHER PEOPLE'S CLARINETS. TRY BEING NICE TO PEOPLE AND THEN MAYBE YOU WILL NOT HAVE TO DRINK GALLONS OF ALCOHOL TO DROWN OUT THE CRAP THAT IS YOUR LIFE. P.P.S. TRY PAYING YOUR FACTORING CHARGE YOU EVIL PLAYBOY AND FUGITIVE

'It is a masterpiece of the genre,' Max admits.

'Andy's an entirely dubgeous character, and you, Maxy-boy, as *aff*orementioned, are a coward.'

* * *

Max-Pedar has cleared the table and loaded the dishwasher, waving away my insincere offers of help. I suddenly have an image of Inga-Bodil, only the second time I ever met her, stacking big china dinner plates on a little trolley, wheeling it through to the dining room table where her husband presided and Max and I sat.

'Every meal an ordeal,' said Duncan, rolling his rs even more scottishly than usual and rubbing his hands, before carving the roast chicken. This was the first time I'd ever gone to stay for the weekend.

'I've put you in separate bedrooms,' Inga-Bodil had whispered the night before, 'because it's more fun with the sneaking about.' She patted my arm. Sol was at my parents' and Max-Pedar and I had been living together for several months by then.

Sneaking about was more tricky than I'd anticipated. The house was huge. Taking a wrong turn emerging from one of the several bathrooms, I got lost in the plush carpeted corridors, opening door after door onto spare rooms and the master bedroom, only managing to orientate myself from the central oak staircase and the polished panelling on the landing. I looked out of the window at the darkened lawns. The extensive, terraced garden, dew- drenched and ghostly in the moonlight, spoke of 1920s tennis parties.

We were all on our third G&T. Inga-Bodil ferried through and laid out dishes of vegetables and crispy roast potatoes, three gravy boats, next to the pressed napkins. As Duncan carved, Inga-Bodil wheeled out the two-tier trolley laden with every kind of bottle, which they called The Alla Cart, parked it next to the table. Max-Pedar took a bottle of wine and gestured at my glass on the table.

'Pick from the à la carte menu,' he grinned. 'You can have what's on the trolley.' We all laughed.

The food was delicious. Inga-Bodil had spent the whole morning in the scullery preparing it, while Duncan was in the study, writing a paper on Enoch Powell to present to the Magdala Debating Society. Since she had insisted that the young people should be outside in the sunshine, we had barely had a conversation all together until now. We were on our second helpings. Though Max had already filled me in, I asked the requisite polite questions about how the two of them had first met.

In the sixties, when Inga-Bodil had come over to Glasgow for an English language summer school. She needed the qualification to take up the next stage of her fashion studies in London. Duncan was fifteen years older, pursuing research into coronary disease, though he'd given that up and taken a consultant's position down South when Max-Pedar was born.

'That must have been interesting,' I said to Duncan, 'the research.'

'Certainly better than being a glorified plumber, as I am now,' he responded, jerking his head in the direction of his wife. 'What did she care? She had her doctor, and her precious boy, and her big fancy house in Mapperley Park.'

Inga-Bodil turned her back, took another helping of roast potatoes and reached for the gravy boat.

'Glutton,' pronounced Duncan audibly.

'My family were farmers in the Arctic many generations,' Inga-Bodil declared, addressing herself pointedly to me. 'Very hard working and good people,' she glared at Duncan, 'but without an interest in couture. Except my mother, she was Swedish – always very stylish. She spelled my name in the Swedish way, Inga not Inger – such trouble I had at school, they would never spell it right – and she made all my clothes herself. Everyone's mothers did, but mine were a little special – just a touch, a ribbon, a pocket, an edging to the collar a little individual, you would say. Always. We didn't say chic then, but it was chic. And she was chic. The way she curled her hair out at the bottom before anyone else. She read magazines but it was like she had instinct. It's very important.' She glared again at Duncan, who ignored her, apparently buried in the draft of his paper which lay beside his plate. 'The female instinct. We women know it's good to eat, to eat nourishing food, the food of life,' she piled my plate with potatoes and began to pour on more gravy, adding a spreading pool to her own plate. 'When we were new married, he ever was complaining I made lumpy gravy, you know, and now he say I eat it all up. Gravy – what a thing is that! And his mince and tatties. He call me the peasant but this is the food of a people without culture, I would say. She poured herself another large splash of gin into her glass, without adding more tonic. Duncan rolled his eyes.

'Where's mine then, woman?' he addressed her back as she went off in search of more lemon. Only when she had filled his glass and added a mite more to her own did she add a splash of tonic from the bottle on the trolley.

'The woman is as fat as a pig and oblivious to her own grossness,' observed Duncan to the room at large. 'She possesses no natural delicacy, so there is nothing whatever to be done.'

'Hey, that's a bit harsh,' I protested, hoping Inga-Bodil hadn't heard and unsure whether I should, as Max was doing, act like this was a joke, or normal dinner-table repartee. Certainly Inga-Bodil was substantially plumper than the slender waif in the hair band and A-line mini-dress in the photograph on the mantelpiece in the snug, but Duncan was rather portly himself. Besides, Inga-Bodil had already made me her female ally.

'I am... woman, and women need gravy...,' Inga-Bodil announced, waggling her wrist and slopping an ice cube onto the carpet, noticing in slow and exaggerated motion just a little too late.

He gave a snort of disgust, then leaned in close and said something right in her ear that I didn't catch. She batted away the arm that held her by the elbow and ran from the room.

Perched on the single bed in Max-Pedar's old room, listening to the sound of pigeons cooing down the chimney, I'd asked him for an explanation. It wasn't like he had concealed anything before that, just that nothing prepared for the reality of it.

'After the last time Dad was sectioned,' Max said, 'he accepted he had to continue with the lithium, but he still objects that it stabilises him at a mood-level lower than he likes. And the trouble with that is... ,' he paused, 'well, the problem is that the depression needs, erm, self-medication.'

I remember Max's voice, as though on the edge of laughter and with a strange excitement in it, telling me of finding his father making hair oil in the Kenwood Chef in the middle of the night, or the founding of The Information Corporation, whose letter-headed notepaper, with the Harley Street address, so many years later supplied reams of scrap paper for Sol and Rosa to draw on. After all, Duncan figured, if he didn't know something himself, he was sure to have a friend or colleague who could supply the answer, a one-man, pre-internet Wikipedia. Those were the good times after all, buying the silver mines in Potosi, Duncan making sure Max and Inga-Bodil knew all about the Bolivian silver market. It all sounded incredibly old-fashioned and colonial to me, hard to believe as having happened only a decade or so before. But then, Duncan used phrases like 'a touch of the tar brush', which seemed to belong to an era so antiquated its racism seemed almost unreal, parodic. He'd even said something of the kind at tea-time.

'My father's mother, she was Sami, a very proud woman,' rejoined Inga-Bodil, with some dignity. 'She would not like to see how he speak to me, how he insult my family, but she is dead. All are dead.' This time, she even put down her G&T to sweep out of the room.

So Max-Pedar always dismissed the idea that our own little fracas were anything much. 'Believe me,' he'd say, 'Nothing our kids have seen compares to what went on in that house.'

* * *

Rosa has headed off to meet Acey and Beccafinlayson. 'If Eilidhnixon shows up, tell her we're in H&M. She's such a flake, she probably won't. She can text us but there's no reception.'

I look out of the window again, to watch her cross the square, almost gambolling as she reaches the statue, curly ponytail bobbing, her long black legs gangly beneath her coat. Still no Ralph. It's not usually a whole day we don't see him.

Rosa quite often stops and chats to Ralph when she's sent out to fetch something from the shop. I'll look out to check for her return and see her standing before him with the shopping bags sagging at her feet, while he sits, puffing on his roll-up, the two of them laughing occasionally. Last week when I looked she was sitting beside him, her non-regulation school skirt puffed out around her, and he had a bruise, a big one, on his cheek, and was not speaking.

'Someone hit him,' she said when she came inside. 'He's got more bruises on his ribs and arms – and no, before you ask, he doesn't want us to tell anyone.'

'Who was it? One of his clients?' Max-Pedar always found it easier to use that word than I would have done.

'No,' Rosa said, 'Ralph said it was a man who owns one of the flats in the next street, where he stands sometimes, someone who doesn't approve of the trade.' She was angry, as she had been about the seagulls, and at the same time proud of her knowledge and the flourish of the last phrase. 'The one with the brown leather jacket and the baldy head – the slap-heid mannie.' She liked that one too.

Well, we'd reached the limits of my ineffectual social work all right. Ralph was an adult and had good reason not to want the police involved. Whom else could we involve anyway? A doctor? More effective social workers? Ralph was too old to be within their jurisdiction, and I'd no idea whether he'd ever been in care. It was up to him what he wanted to do, and it seemed he wanted to do nothing in this case. Imperfect, like all his choices, like all choices, mine included, made not with some overarching view but with little knowledge of the future, one at a time Max-Pedar turns down my offer to wash up the coffee cups. 'I've got a bit more to do on those shots. Sorry to be so anti-social. Do you have some stuff to do?' Later, he'll want to talk it through, the rationale for the book, the ordering, the font design. Even though I love his photographs, I'm dreading it.

Sure I do. I should be filling in the application form for the ceramics access course, or that'll be another year gone. God knows, I've worked in the admissions office long enough to know the process. Not that I can afford to do it, even if I get in. 'I think I'll have a bath.'

The water is slightly cloudy from all the shampoo Rosa uses. Watching it creep over my belly, the milky swirls forming and reforming, I try to think about what I need for the application. Instead I think about Ari, Sol's father, the reason I had to leave Art College the first time. We were children ourselves, then, really. It wasn't the pregnancy, the child, which so changed the world for me. It was the completeness with which, even before he knew, Ari had turned his back on me. I stopped attending classes, couldn't come across him in a corridor, at the bus stop, without dissolving into tears. I was manipulating everyone, making them sorry for me, he said, making them blame him. It was disgusting. Who did I think I was? He was in the year below me, transferred that summer and moved away, just weeks before Sol was born.

For a long while after, I could tell just by looking at people how they felt about their bodies. It was as if I'd drunk a potion, like the ones in children's stories that enable you to understand the animals, only for me it unlocked the secrets of sexual confidence, physical fear. This person thinks that no one should ever see her thighs with the light on, this one, despite all assurances, sees every crease of his sagging skin through the eyes of his new, young partner. I assumed it was because Ari, my first and only lover, had rejected me so comprehensively and so soon. To my enormous surprise, this person who had seemed to love me so much had not wanted my body, or the fruits of my body.

Running into him so unexpectedly in Carlisle Station after all those years... It had never occurred to me his parents probably still lived in Penrith. I was changing trains, coming back from a funeral. Aunty Maureen from the library. I'd gone for Mum really, her oldest friend. Emotional occasion. Perhaps that was why. We had a drink, though only one, I always maintain, in the station bar, and I caught a later train. Killing an hour walking the damp streets, I was surprised how easy it was to chat, to talk about my life, about Sol, the boy he'd never seen. He had a daughter, seven years old, whom he did see regularly, though separated from her mother. As we approached the platform, he pulled me towards him and kissed me.

'You still smell the same,' he said. 'Exactly the same.'

So, contrary to the expectations of Inga-Bodil, who'd always confidently and rather racily, in her Scandinavian way, expected her son to be the one to stray if I didn't watch my step, it was me who had the affair. Despite all the guilt, I discovered I enjoyed the lying, the perfection of the double bluff. Max knew all about how enlivened I was by this renewed acquaintance with Ari, how important the connection for Sol. Everything in the open, hiding in plain sight. We only met up twice, once in a bed and breakfast place up the coast, and once down in London, when I claimed to be going to a ceramics exhibition. It wasn't just the delight of being desired, the excitement – I don't imagine I could have been unfaithful to Max-Pedar with someone new, but Ari had a prior claim – a prior claim to be told where to get off, probably, but I always was a sucker for redemption. We talked about what had happened, he was remorseful, I was forgiving: he wanted me, he had come back. I even got some kind of retrospective reassurance by way of explanation:

'It was the sex – I was too young, I guess you were too but I just thought about me. You were my first girlfriend, and I felt I was so crap at it... yes, I know, you wouldn't have known... you didn't have anything to compare either, and you were lovely about it, but I was rubbish, and I knew... I knew you would realise and then you'd leave me.'

'So you left me first?' I was incredulous, but apparently that's a thing. A thing everybody knows about but me.

He and Sol had a few lengthy phone calls, and skyped for a while, talked of meeting up. Then Ari disappeared again. He had a new young girlfriend he'd met at a festival where he did stage design.

When I tracked him down and he told me, it was as though I'd inhaled in a single, never-ending gulp all the pain of the first time, and this one, and that I couldn't speak, would never speak again. Except that this time, I should have known better. This time I'd had a choice. I managed one sentence more than the first time around, at least – only one, and a question:

'Is this it – do you have to be so... so monumentally inadequate?'
Of course he did.

I'd said all along and very firmly that I'd never leave Max-Pedar
and break up the family, so I guess I wasn't offering much. What
did I learn – apart from the fact that I was an utter fool – that Ari
couldn't help it? He couldn't help it the first time, and he couldn't the
second. If he could have, he would. I genuinely believe that. It didn't
excuse him one iota. Or me either. It was just a fact. And, after Max-
Pedar found out, and all the recriminations and the reconciliation
and the two years of trying again, I discovered that I could break up
a family, my family, after all.

The under-floor heating in the bathroom is gentle on my hot feet.
Woozy from the steam, I make myself dress in my slightly damp
clothes and creep into the hallway. Max has his back to me, still bent
over the breakfast bar. I unlock the door silently and head down
the stairs, desperate for fresh air. From the top step I see the seated
figure in the dark grey hoodie, his white converse trainers crossed
in front of him.

* * *

I go and sit on the wee wall and, though I've never been a smoker,
accept when Ralph offers me a cigarette. He has a packet, for once,
Marlboro Golds. We don't really talk. I feel I should, but mainly
need to concentrate on remembering how to smoke. I realise I'm
imitating some long-ago memory of Ari as I try to rest my thumb
against my cheekbone, but when I glance to the side I see that Ralph
is in the same pose.

'I prefer roll-ups to be honest with ye, ken?'

'I haven't smoked since before my son was born, and even then it
wasn't... I mean only occasionally, other people's... like now. I never
bought my own.'

'Best way,' he grins. His teeth are white but slightly transparent,
as if his overall purple tinge lurks beneath the enamel. Quite gappy
teeth. Small, very regular. Unlike his fingers, not tobacco stained.
What do I look like to him, I wonder? Frumpy, well-meaning,
middle-aged wifie. I haven't cleaned my teeth, run my furry tongue

160

over a back molar. It feels like I've just eaten rhubarb.

We've got past the stage in the conversation where I'd have to open with 'how's it going?' A question with too many awkward inferences to be comfortable with, for me at least, which is why I've been nursing it, unsaid. Looking upward, I see Andy at his top floor window. He has it wide open so his straggly hair blows across his face, a hungover smile visible even from here, a rueful wave of salutation. I wave back. Ralph nods. I can't see an air-rifle.

'Did yer daughter gie him the letter, like? Aboot the seagulls.'

'Oh yeah, well no, she gave it to her Dad – I think he's censored it.'

'Mebbe jist as weel. It wis a bittie strang.'

'Did you see it? Did you tell her?'

'Aye, right enough. That letter'd a tellt him though, eh?' He turns to me and his shoulders shake with a silent chuckle.

'That's for sure.'

We look each other in the eye as though balancing our joint appreciation of Rosa on the gossamer thread of our gaze. His eyes are dark brown and a little bloodshot, the pupils small. If I expect them to be pools of sadness, I'm disappointed.

'Can I get you a cuppa?' I've tried not to be ungrateful by stubbing out the cigarette with an unseemly long fag-end. I want to stay out here in the weak sunshine on the lumpy wall, not go back into the flat, where Max-Pedar will look up, and want to talk to me about what he's working on – which is often interesting, but not really voluntary since I have to, because of the dinner I've just received, and usually makes me agitated about my own incomplete tasks, like the application, which I'm still avoiding. It's rarely helpful to talk any of my own things through with Max-Pedar – since it's always so clear to him either that I should be doing something different or doing what I am doing entirely differently.

I'm still useful to him as a sounding board, though, and always just a step away from the accusation of not taking an interest. It's the least I can do, after all. And it's something we are good at, together, and time will pass, and he'll talk and talk, till the warmth of the room and the fug of seduction envelop me, and I know I'll stay, and that if I stay I'll have to make a fight of it at bedtime, when every pore of my skin is screeching 'for fuck's sake!' Because I can't be bothered to go home, to the cold and untidy house I don't have the energy to make more than acceptably tidy, with my bedroom full of boxes and every room too full of his stuff, and my stuff and the children's stuff. There's too much of everything and I can't find any of it, so that, though I have a fear of losing the least shred of it, every day when I lock the door to take Rosa to school, part of me reflects that it would be relief if some electrical fault caused the whole place to burn down.

* * *

I decide to walk. I say goodbye to Ralph, and head off down the backstreets towards the Cathedral, moving briskly to compensate for not having brought a coat. Max Pedar thinks sex is a human right.

'Why not?' he'll demand. 'You'll dry up without it. Wither. You know you will. It's not healthy. Now we don't live together, we don't have any problems really, do we? We get on really well. Go on. Meaningless as you like.'

'You should have more self-respect,' I'll charge him, which is ironic really.

'It's only until one of us gets a better offer,' he'll counter. Until he does, he means. 'We know each other so well, after all – it's not like it wouldn't be bloody nice...'

I say: 'It's like telling someone at the end of an interview that they haven't got the job and they just say "I'll start Monday then, shall I?"'

'It's hard to respect decisions I know aren't in your best interests. I still love *you*, remember?'

Perhaps it's because I remember being on the receiving end, I lack Ari's forensic cruelty – I can't make it stick. That, I suddenly realise, is why Ari needed to be so cruel, both times, to make it final, to make me give up.

As for Max-Pedar, he'll start Monday.

I walk faster, taking random turns down unfamiliar streets. I'm probably going in a circle but I don't care. If Max has come to a break in his work, he'll have realised by now that I'm gone, and he has had several kirs, but what can I do? I can't start hiding in *his* bathroom, after all. That was the first sign, well before the Ari fiasco, when I first began locking myself in the bathroom for long periods. It felt as though there was nowhere to go, nowhere to be that Max-Pedar didn't reach, with his endless descriptions, of the world, of me. He noticed but, unusually, did not add this behaviour to his list of charges of dereliction of duty.

'You need to get away from the kids,' was his explanation.

Rosa was six, and the house was always full of her friends from school and the neighbours' children. It was true but I knew he realised that was not the real or the full reason. After years of resisting the idea, he agreed we should have some couple counselling.

'I just need a referee,' I said. 'You always conduct your side of the argument *and* control the terms on which we're allowed to have it. It's exhausting. Once in a blue moon I manage to battle through and persuade you to see things another way, but it just takes so much... so much insight and eloquence, so much *energy*. And you seem to accept things, just for a while and it's such a relief when you seem to *see* – but it doesn't change anything. I need a referee,' I repeated lamely.

The counselling woman was pleasant, in her mid-forties, softly spoken and almost apologetic, with lightly curled hair. I saw how much effort Max-Pedar was making, for I noted him register that Lois was not cleverer than him, and that, in his mind, she belonged to the well-meaning, lower-middle-classes. He hadn't used to be like that, I remember thinking. Was this really the man I was supposed to have turned into a dungaree-clad, socialist hippie? Who knew there were so many categories of the bourgeoisie anyway? Max-Pedar was sure he could 'cure' himself, through his own self-reflection and reading, if I would only concur with him in removing the environmental stresses and triggers. He was coming to counselling for *me*.

Lois, to her credit, was a faithful referee, and it was a relief to be able to try and say what I felt and what I wanted without polemic. It was also not a little enjoyable to see Max-Pedar disorientated at not being able to shape the discussion.

'I feel like there are so many words,' Lois said wearily at the end of the second session. 'It's as if the air in the room is filled with them, floating about like balloons. And you,' she said to Max-Pedar '– this is not in any sense a judgement, but it seems as if you're up there on the ceiling.' Max-Pedar laughed uncomfortably, shrugged, went into analytical mode, spinning more words, but Lois cut him off. 'I'm sorry to interrupt you, Max,' she said, 'but how does it feel to hear that?'

The counselling was discontinued when Max-Pedar walked out of the third session and would not go back. I had mentioned the hitting. It was a breach of our agreement, apparently.

'So it's my fault – yet another contract I'm not aware I've signed? How bad was it anyway? All she said was "I'm sorry to hear there's been violence between you." It wasn't like there was going to be a big blame scenario and we might've got to actually talk about it. I'm quite happy to admit to hitting you back.'

I knew why I'd brought it up, though. By the third session, Max-Pedar thought he'd got the measure of Lois. He'd started doing the one thing I couldn't stomach – pretending to be a normal person. The good boy.

'I won't be seen as some wife-beater – you're the one who first crossed the threshold of violence, remember? She'd have to see that.'

That had always been the claim. The first incident had occurred soon after Rosa was born. We were in the kitchen of the little rented flat near Max-Pedar's office. The baby was in my arms, peeking over my shoulder, just two or three months old, entranced by a picture we had pinned to the cupboard door. Max-Pedar had been criticising me a lot lately, I felt. I was great with the baby, even he admitted that, but I had a tendency to stack up the dishes by the sink and head out to feed the ducks in the park, to visit cafes or other women from the ante-natal classes, to walk endlessly, pushing the pram, collecting Sol from school and heading to the playground again, returning as near to the hour of Max-Pedar's homecoming as I could. When Sol was born, I had gone back to Yorkshire, to family and old school friends with babies. I didn't recall the sensation of the dragging hours, of being stuck in my house by myself – with a baby who, delightful as she was, could be entertained and grow up anywhere, and who enjoyed being out and about even more than I did.

'Motherhood, and the whole housewife thing, they're two

different jobs really,' I said. 'I'm really good at *one* of them.'

'Other women manage,' Max-Pedar pointed out. 'What is it you want? You couldn't ask for a more hands-on father than me. I gave up a whole week when she was born, and I've taken time off to work at home. I don't have to do that – I'm not supposed to, in fact. I'm contractually obliged, you know. The other guys there don't do that, and my boss wouldn't like it if he knew how much I...'

'Then there's something wrong with the culture at your work and you don't need to go along with it.'

'I even give her a bath every morning so you can sleep in a bit. I'm forever picking up Sol from school. And I do far more in the house than most blokes. '

'Yeah, that's just it – you... you think you're doing me such a big favour – cause it's *really my job*! We're not living in a sodding Ladybird book!'

He'd been standing beside me, having pointedly finished the last of the dishes left from the night before.

'My dad did nothing – my mother had him to deal with, as well as me to look after and she didn't com...'

'She had *help*,' I hissed, 'a string of *au pairs*, and a woman who did the laundry. She told me herself. Said she'd never have...' I wanted to yell but instead stroked the soft stubble of Rosa's dark hair over her neat and perfect scalp, inhaling deeply. She gave a gurgle, fiddling intently with a button on my nightie then riveting her gaze on something over my shoulder once more, her eyes liquid pools of blackness, tracing the repeated geometric shapes of the brown-and-yellow wallpaper next to the cooker.

He leaned in close:

'Not all men would put up with it,' he said, 'a snappy, spotty, sexless lump with a floppy stomach and clothes stinking of puke....'

I was close enough to grasp his arm below the elbow and squeeze hard. It was a deliberate pinch, no doubt about it, even though it felt like I was simply crushing the rage and pain he had just occasioned back into him, but I was conscious that I didn't want the baby to see such unpleasantness and childish behaviour from her parents. He punched me so hard on the upper arm that I went flying, landing awkwardly in the rocking chair I used for breastfeeding, which luckily still contained a pillow. My other hand was able to come up and protect Rosa's head so she landed against my shoulder with a bit of a bump and a squawk of surprise but nothing worse. Aware of my own disbelief, soaking through my bare feet into the cold lino, I felt the corner of the metal guard around the gas fire digging into my knee.

Why couldn't I at least have had one of those remorseful ones, I often thought afterwards, full of broken promises never, ever to do it again? But no, crossing the threshold of violence – even if it was only throwing a baby's sponge bath-book in his direction – that was provocation, whereas his uttering the most unbearable, unsayable thing imaginable, in his low voice, right next to my ear, was not. Until the time when Rosa was four and he'd punched me in the back lying face down in bed because I'd spent too much time talking to some American guy who, according to Max-Pedar, was plainly lusting after me, at his works party. The threshold of violence pretence was dropped, mostly, after that – though Max-Pedar always declared that occasion an anomaly.

To be fair, it didn't happen very often – say once every six months or a year. I was good at dodging and running just as the punch was thrown, and usually thumped him back if the kids weren't around. Max-Pedar was always adamant that it wasn't because I'd finally said to him – 'if you hit me one more time I'm leaving and I'm taking Sol and Rosa with me' – that things changed. No, it was because one day, mending the door of the rabbit hutch in the back garden, he'd risen to hit me, infuriated by something I'd said as I put down the mug of tea on the out-house step beside him. We must've been arguing earlier, though I've no recollection of the subject of the dispute. There were so many by then and yet they were all the same, just one continuous topic of retribution and disappointment.

Max-Pedar liked practical tasks and was undoubtedly rather good at them. This one must have been taking a while, though, because Rosa was no longer 'helping' and had taken the rabbit upstairs to play with on her bed. The chicken wire wasn't compliant, or there wasn't quite enough of it. I took one look at his face and the hammer in his hand and bolted for the back door, through the kitchen, falling over myself on the way upstairs. He stood at the bottom of the stairs, at the very place in the hallway where he'd once ripped my favourite poster from the wall and on another occasion kicked out a pane of glass in the door to the kitchen in front of a wailing Rosa and stone-faced Sol. I picked myself up and sat at a safe distance on the top stair, rubbing the carpet burn on my knee, unsure what was holding him back. I could hear Rosa conducting a squeaky two-way conversation with the rabbit. Sol had his music on. If I could diffuse this one, they might not have to witness anything. Max-Pedar's arms dangled awkwardly by his sides and his face had an odd, unresolved expression I'd not seen before.

'Are you afraid of me?' he asked. 'Physically afraid, I mean.'

'Of course I fucking am, you total arse-hole. Some enraged bloke is running after me waving a hammer – which part of you doesn't realise how terrifying that is? How fucking delusional, how completely stupid *are* you?'

So much for defusing the situation, but my own fury and disbelief that I was being asked to *persuade* him of my fear swept through me like adrenaline. How had he not known? I suppose my tendency to land him one back might've been misleading all those years. And as for the marks on my back and arms, never on my face, I bruised easily, he always said. Nothing to do with the severity of the blows. At some point I deliberately calmed myself enough to utter the immortal words about leaving and taking the children, but it wasn't that, he assured me later, which altered everything. We couldn't even agree on that.

Still, he stopped. I pushed my luck and walloped him a few times after that, enjoying my impunity, because he was as good as his word. I wasn't grateful, just angry. As if he'd said: 'I don't need to hit you. I just like to.' Having had to *talk* him into stopping galled me beyond measure. I wished I could've picked up the plinth of the rabbit hutch door and hit him and hit him and hit him. It frightened me. If he could discover such restraint now, he could've stopped any time he wanted.

* * *

I stride past Private Eyes with its blacked-out windows, its cocktail and masked eyes graphic, with some tagline about gentlemen in a gold, cursive script. I've been pounding the pavements so hard and so fast my feet hurt and I'm sweating. I come into the square just as Rosa crosses the car park from the other side. I wave. At least we can go in together.

Max is in a good mood, sitting in the armchair listening to his latest Lucinda Williams CD with the last of bottle of white in his glass. He obviously got done what he needed to without me.

'I made some open sandwiches with the leftover ham, if you're peckish, he says. They're in the fridge. Oh, and there are choc-ices for later.'

Rosa dives into the freezer section. I'm not hungry but nibble a sandwich, turn down more wine. We start the process of selecting a DVD to watch. Rosa and Max favour *Miss Congeniality II*. It's just beginning to get dark.

Hazel comes sweeping into the flat, spray tan immaculate, her hair in a high, blond ponytail, 'Hello, pet,' to Rosa, who's answered the door. 'Well he's done it now.'

'Who has?'

'That's him coming back now,' she gestures out of the window.

'Not the seagulls,' says Rosa menacingly. 'I'll kill him.'

'I caught him on the corner – I'd just popped out to buy a paper – and he told me. Here he is now – he can tell you himself,' and she dives back out of the door and down the stairs.

Andy's pale raincoat is flapping around him, the belt too long on one side, the other end about to drop out at of its loop at any moment. He's puffing and his hair is all over the place, his expression half-sheepish, half radiant.

'Go on, then,' Hazel urges. 'Tell em, pet.'

'Well, I just said, when I saw im, I said. "Do you know where you are? Do you know *where you are*? We don't do that ere." And e didn't say nuffin, like, like e'd no idea what I was on abaht. So I said "the boy, the boy like – covered in bruises, covered in em. We don't do that ere, mate, you know that." And e didn't say nuffin, so I nutted im. The bald geezer, you know, the one wiv the fancy jacket.'

Max-Pedar brings out The Magic Roundabout and reaches in the cupboard for more glasses. Rosa is full of it, eyes dark with excitement – 'Is he ok? You didn't kill him, did you?' – but it's clear the seagull-slayer has redeemed himself in her big, round eyes.

The clock spire of St Mary's is blackened by the greyness of evening, the frothy crowns of the chestnut trees dusted by the light from the first street lamps. A seagull perches dimly on the pallid head of Lord Gordon's statue. There is no sign of Ralph. I don't need to ask Rosa whether she wants to stay over at her Dad's tonight, with so much drama and its aftermath to soak up, with Hazel leaning over confidentially to tell her something, and asking her about her dancing. Andy is apologising for making too much noise when he came in late the other night. Max-Pedar is pouring him another Laphroaig.

Pressing just behind my eyes, is a thought that has been in the back of my mind ever since we started taking out tea to the rent boy but refused to coalesce, the thought that it isn't just Ralph who sells himself too cheaply. I am grateful for the food and the pleasant surroundings and the warmth, but suddenly I have found the energy to go home, empty fridge, haywire central heating and all. Max-Pedar is so caught up in all the hilarity and hospitality that he hasn't got around to asking me to stay, not yet switched into seduction mode, though with the gin and tonics he's downing, it will be instantaneous the minute Rosa is in bed and everyone has gone. I don't wait, but retrieve my coat from the hall and slip downstairs to the waiting car.

Acknowledgements

THIS COLLECTION WAS COMPLETED WITH THE HELP OF a generous Writer's Bursary from Creative Scotland, for which I'm extremely grateful. Some of these stories, or versions of them, first appeared in other publications – 'Sapozhkelekh' in *The Interpreter's House* (2016), 'Starred Man' in *Causeway/Cabshair* (2014),'Overnight Observation' in *The Year of Open Doors* (Glasgow: Cargo Press, 2010),'French Leave' in *Even More Tonto Short Stories* (Newcastle: Tonto, 2010), 'The Mintie Wifie' in *Gutter Magazine* (2009), and 'Half-Mast' in *Cheatin' Hearts: Women's Secret Stories* (London: Serpent's Tail, 2000) – and I would like to express my gratitude to their editors here for allowing these tales their first foray into the world.

For their ever-fruitful scrutiny of the work in progress and their much-needed encouragement, I am thankful to Konstancja Duff, Alan Spence, Kenneth Stephen and Martin Walsh. Thanks also to Sheena Blackhall, Geordie Murison, Stanley Robertson and Kate Taylor for the Doric, while my appreciation goes, likewise and in memoriam, to Sister Angèle Quizet. Acknowledgement is due to Marie de France, Chrétien de Troyes, Silvia Federici, John Milton and a host of sixteenth and seventeenth-century misogynists for some handy ideas, as well as to that cluster of colleagues who managed to impart some productive working practices and stress-reduction strategies: Sasha Schell, Aine Larkin, Marsaili Macleod, Hazel Hutchison and Silvia Casini. According to proverb, gratitude is the heart's memory, so I recall here Miriam and Jasmine Duff, Susan Marshall, Sergio Domingo Braz and Alec Macdonald, Timothy Baker, Claire White, Anne Taylor, Eileen Bresnan, Peter and Lynn Saunders, Dave Wilkie, and Drew and Helen Riach, for ensuring I have somewhere lovely to live, and that my house doesn't fall down.

Thanks to the staff of *Bella Italia* at the beach – Boris Borisov, Gosia Janczar, Ana Paz Perez, Martin Puentes and Steve Ross – to Val and Calum at *Buchanan's*, and to Martin and Sarah at *The Pier Bistro*, for the cosy and conducive writing habitats, and regular flow of caffeine; Also to Gabriela Wagner and family (including Birk and Jon Snow) for the perfect annual Nordic retreat. I'm also very grateful to Adrian Searle at Wild Harbour Press for his continuing belief in this enterprise, as well as to Darren Gate and Angela Docherty for precision, flair and tact in the process of publication.

As always and most often, I am indebted to family, to friends and fellow-musicians for much love and support, and many pleasant distractions.